THINGS THAT GO
UNSPOKEN

THINGS THAT GO UNSPOKEN

Antonella Lattanzi

Translated from the Italian by
Jamie Richards

LONDON

'Le bombe delle sei non fanno male,
è solo il giorno che muore.'

Antonello Venditti, 'Notte prima degli esami'

One

We went up to Circeo, even though it was the most absurd thing to do. The most dangerous.

We've been out of our minds for a while. Months. We've been out of our minds, and it feels as if the world is out of its mind along with us. The doctors, the few friends who know, and the others – most of the people we know and love – who have no idea what's going on.

We went up to Circeo, where there's no phone signal, where there's no wi-fi, where terrible things happened not so long ago, up there on the cape. The rocks jut out at you, tall and raw, as you climb or descend the hairpin bends, and you know you're all alone. If there's an emergency, you're alone. If you die, you're alone.

I lie down on the bed, next to Andrea, but I'm terrified. The bed is pushed into the corner of the seaside cottage we picked out back in March when everything had just happened, and we didn't know it could get any worse. This corner where the bed is wedged looms over me, just like the cape where we're hiding out, unable to communicate with anyone. The terror I feel is bigger and blacker than the cliffs.

Andrea picks up a book. I listen to what's happening to my body. I can feel the blood flowing out of me, as it has since February. Now it's June. Blood in drops, gobs, spurts, buckets. Now it comes out of me liquid and infinite as I lie outstretched and try not to breathe. Maybe, I tell myself, if you hold your breath the bleeding will stop.

I can't admit to Andrea how scared I am or he'll say, let's go back to Rome.

And I can't do that. I can't give in. I don't want to give in to all this pain. I want my June in Circeo, I have a right to try to put my life back together, a right to sit on the smooth-worn rocks and stare out at the sea without feeling pain in every part of my body. I have a right to say, I reject everything that happened, I reject reality, I reject that this could happen to me. That it is happening to me. I don't want to come to terms with what happened. I want it not to have happened at all.

I'm lying on the bed. A bigger, longer gush soaks my pad. I turn towards Andrea. 'How's it going?' he asks.

But he already knows. Because I turned to look at him, he knows.

'Blood,' I say.

I want to cry and tell him how scared I am. I want to tell him, take me to Rome, take me to the hospital. But I can't. If you pretend there isn't blood everywhere, there won't be. I say 'blood' as if I were saying 'sorry'.

'How much?' he says.

This responsibility I have, that only I can have, to know how much blood I'm losing, whether it's *too much*, is driving me crazy. No one can help me to tell how much blood this is.

'Maybe not that much,' I lie. 'Can't we go to sleep?'

It's June and I haven't slept in months, night or day. Months after this, I still won't be able to sleep. I'll wake up at one, two, three, four, every night. I'll never nap during the day. Is it possible to bleed to death without realising?

'I don't know,' he says. 'Only you can tell.'

He searches my face. Only I can tell *how much* blood it is. Whether it's too much. ('Bleeding is serious,' my gynaecologist said. 'Try to manage if you can. But if it doesn't stop, get yourself to A&E'). But how much is *too much*? If someone cuts themselves by accident, and the bleeding doesn't stop, they consider going to hospital. If I think of it this way, the bleeding has been too much for months. February, March, April, May, June. All that time popping haemostatics. Six 500 mg tablets of Tranex a day. The maximum dose. Sometimes, I secretly take three or four more. Vials are better, I know, the drug works faster: it starts circulating right after you drink it. But vials are glass and they shatter in my hands because I'm always trembling when I open them. My whole body is trembling, head to toe, as if I were epileptic, as if I couldn't stop dancing. At the hospital they tell me Tranex shouldn't be taken for months on end, it's very dangerous.

Dictionary. Word: *danger*. Antonym: *safety*. But that's not the case for me. In these past months, the word 'danger' has taken on another opposite: survival. Between danger and survival, I have no choice but survival. Day by day, hour by hour. I don't stop to think about all the dangers. I can't. Blood doesn't care what medications I take. My blood doesn't care about anything. It flows.

'How much blood?' he asks.

'I don't know,' I reply.

'What do you want to do? Should we go back to Rome?'

I'm the one who has to decide. No one can decide for me, and it's not because they don't want to. It's that no one else is inside my body. We're in Circeo because I wanted to go. Because I demanded to go. I wish I had some way of measuring how many millilitres of blood I'm losing, or litres, to tell me whether it's OK. That this much is acceptable.

But if Andrea asks me should we go back to Rome, the only answer is no. Rome means admitting what's going on. Rome means A&E and an inevitable operation with even more risk.

'No,' I say.

'You sure?'

'I'm sure.'

My pounding heart is breaking my sternum. Everything hurts. My legs, my arms, my back, my belly, my head. And I feel weak, so very weak. My haemoglobin keeps falling, and despite the iron, folic acid, vitamin B, and vitamin D, despite the transfusions, despite the haemostatics, it continues to drop. I can't go up an incline. Or take a walk. I'm winded just going from the bedroom to the bathroom. My heart races if I so much as pick up a pair of shoes.

'Could you stay awake for a little while?' I ask.

My head is telling me, you're crazy, get back to Rome, go to A&E, you can't even take a breath without bleeding. I lift the sheet and in terror pull down my underwear. I don't want to look, but I have to. No one can do it for me. I look down. Red. Bright red. Even with a stack of four incontinence pads, the sheets end up stained. I have to sleep in pants, with a towel wrapped around my body. Not that I'll sleep.

'Of course,' he says. 'But are you sure we don't have to go?'

It's an insane question. No one would hole themselves up in Circeo without wi-fi, without reception, without any means of communication, an hour and a half from Rome, the unpaved, unlit Pontina the only way back to the city. No one. Except us. Except me.

We're crazy. I've always been crazy, Andrea never. But now my madness has infected him.

'Yes,' I say.

'All right.'

We're crazy together, and I eventually close my eyes, he closes his and turns off the light. I've always had monsters in my head. But now they're not monsters. They're living tissue of jellylike blood, globs I can feel coming out of me. And I don't want what's coming out of me to be blood. It can't be real. It's not real.

We close our eyes, we're crazy together, and it's pure luck that I keep nodding off and waking up again, over and over, that night in Circeo, as the sound of the sea, which I've always loved, crescendos ominously. It's pure luck that I don't sleep a moment too long. It's pure luck that in all those months, February, March, April, May, June of 2021, I don't sleep a moment too long. That would be the moment I die in a pool of my own bright red blood.

Two

The story begins when I finally decide.

I never thought about the two babies I aborted.

Now that I keep going back over it – five, I can't not think that it's *five* children I don't have – even now, every time I'm alone with my partner I want to tell him that I should have protected them, taken care of them, loved them; that's what a parent does, that's what a mother does; I should have protected them from scraped knees, from the pain of their first tooth, from stomach aches and sore throats from their first conflicts with other kids; I should have protected them from the cold, I should have protected them from the heat, taking them to the beach in the early morning or late afternoon, slathering them with sunblock so they don't burn, teaching them that the sea is good, it's a friend, that dogs are good, they're friends (but I should have protected them from dogs too, explained that they're not toys, that when a dog comes up to you, first you should put your hand under its chin, palm open, to show that you won't hurt it, let it sniff you, watch its face, see whether it wags its tail or if it stiffens, since not all dogs are the same and not all dogs like being petted); I should have introduced them to the place I'm from and hoped they loved it, I should have shown them, this is Grandpa, this is Grandma (too painful to imagine my parents' overjoyed faces if I'd told them: I'm pregnant, I'm pregnant, I'm pregnant,

I'm pregnant, I'm pregnant, five times – whereas I didn't tell them even once). I should have protected them from fear of the dark, fear of death, fear of my death, fear of their parents dying; I should have explained to them what my father explained to me, when I felt scared of eternal life as we'd been taught about it in church (I would never have taken them to church, so maybe they would only have been scared of death, but eternal life and death are the same thing), I should have told them, as my father had me, that as long as someone is there to remember us, we don't die, and how those words so consoled me that I remember them still. His words, from my mouth, would have consoled my children as I, like a good mum, tucked them into bed. Even now that I think I'm a terrible mother because instead of protecting my children I had a part in what killed them, I never think of the two babies I aborted.

Or rather, I never used to.

I didn't think about them because the thought was too big. I didn't want to be, in the present, the product of every harm I had suffered or caused in the past. I didn't think about them because I didn't want to give a name to these children I didn't have. Because I don't want to think about how old they would be now, or now. Because I don't want a place to go to remember them. I didn't think about them because when other people – friends, acquaintances, colleagues – revealed their own abortion, it brought back my own story. I wanted to say, I know, I understand. I decided to have an abortion. Not once, but twice. It was on the tip of my tongue and always so close to coming out. But I couldn't let it. If you give such a big part of yourself to someone else, how can you protect yourself? If you give away the deepest parts of yourself, they hurt more. Because from that moment on, they exist.

I never thought about them.

I never thought I was the kind of person who doesn't talk about themselves. I didn't think of myself that way. Now I know that I am. That I have a dam in my mind holding back all the things that are too painful. I don't want to tell anybody about those things. I don't want to think about them. I don't want them ever to have existed. And if I don't talk about them, they don't exist.

And then, even on the rare occasions that I do want to talk, how could I? My closest friends, the ones I call family, have no idea. How could I, after knowing them for decades, come out and say, by the way, here's this important thing I never told you?

How would they look at me? Would they think: why wouldn't you tell me something like that?

And how could I explain?

Revealing painful secrets ruins the mood of an evening spent chatting with a close friend over a bottle of wine.

How can the conversation get back to work, love life, sex, fears, joys, if I throw pain like that at someone?

Being sad bores me. I hate it.

I never told anyone. The only ones who know are the fathers of those children.

All this was a factor, it's true. But there was also the shame. When I went to the gynaecologist for a check-up they would ask: any previous pregnancies?

No.

Miscarriages or abortions?

Me, confidently: No.

When I went to other doctors, they would ask: previous surgeries?

No.

Ever undergone general anaesthesia?

No.

You shouldn't lie to doctors, Andrea always tells me. Why go to the doctor, what do you pay them for if you're going to tell them lies?

I always lie to doctors.

What your reason clearly tells you, what you believe in and defend – that getting an abortion doesn't make you a monster – is loudly contradicted by a voice shouting inside you.

You're a monster and you don't want anybody else to know it.

Voluntary interruption of pregnancy is a right; my mother taught me that. But the fact that I've exercised that right is something I can't tell my same mother.

I know that it's a right and I believe in it. And yet when everything that happened happened, and even before, when I finally decided that I wanted to start trying for a child, and for years when that child never came, the thought of those two babies became constant. I couldn't help but conclude that I had brought this tragedy on myself.

In times of suffering we always look for a reason. Why did what happened happen? Because life isn't to be messed with, answered an ancestral voice, the voice of magical thinking. You rejected two lives. And so you have been punished. Another three lives have been taken from you, all at once, because you didn't deserve them. You don't deserve to be a mother.

I couldn't help but reply: you're right.

So why am I telling this story now?

I who never tell anyone anything.

I'm telling it because at this point I can think of nothing else. Nothing but this bright red.

At Christmas in 2020, we went to my friend Giulia's. We spent Christmas Eve with her, her partner Roberto, and their two small children. At the time, I thought I was carrying twins.

I wasn't happy that day. Looking at Giulia, Roberto and their children, I saw what I was going to become – and I was terrified. I don't know how to do this, I thought. I can't do this.

Later, after everything happened, a secret voice told me: that's also why you deserved it. Because instead of dreaming happy dreams of mothers and children and cuddles and breastfeeding and buggies, you had nightmares about not being able to work. You said: no, breastfeeding isn't for me. I can't, I have to be free, I have to be able to work.

Why did you wake up scared every morning? Why were you so terrified you wouldn't be able to write? Why weren't you happy?

This is also why you, with your inability to be a happy mother, deserved what happened.

That Christmas Eve, Andrea, my partner, is shucking oysters in the kitchen with Roberto. We hear a commotion and can tell that something is wrong. Andrea has cut himself, and there's blood, lots of blood. They try to hide it from me because I'm pregnant and don't want me to get scared. But I go into the kitchen and see the blood, and Andrea pressing a rag over his hand.

'Don't you think you should go to hospital?' Roberto asks him.

'No,' Andrea replies.

We wait, worried, for the bleeding to stop, and after a while, it does. They eat the oysters – well, that's not true, I'm lying, and when I'm writing I can't lie: I eat some too – and we sing Christmas songs. I don't say no to a glass or two of wine, because I was never a good mother. Everything repulses me, which makes Giulia laugh. 'That's normal,' she says. 'You're pregnant!' She's so happy for me.

I'm afraid all the time. I feel like there's a plexiglass window between me and the world, and everyone on the other side is living it up, laughing and singing, while I'm stuck behind the glass with my breasts aching, nauseous, overwhelmed by my sense of smell. I can't sleep. I'm never tired. I don't have those charmed naps, the sweet mummy-to-be. I have a reaction to being a mother. But why, if I had willed it to happen, with all my might, for years?

Giulia is excited and has been at my side this whole journey, ever since Andrea and I decided to have a baby four years ago and tried every possible way. Giulia has been with me through it all, even more than Andrea. More than anyone. She's the first person I told about my positive test, not Andrea. I never told my family – not my father, mother, sister. They never knew me pregnant. Not even afterwards. To them, everything that happened never happened.

We sing, we dance, Andrea's cut stops bleeding – it's a wrenching Christmas, frightening and blinding. To think that almost a year has gone by since I couldn't stand the smells and tastes I'd always loved, that now another

Christmas is around the corner, Christmas 2021, when I was supposed to be a mother, had been assured that I would be a mother – to think of everything that was and that is no more, what do I do? What can I do?

When Andrea cuts himself on the oyster, it looks like too much blood to all of us. If only I knew then how much you and I, my dear blood, would be seeing of each other. How much that limit of *too much* blood would go up and up, every day, in the months to come. When I think about it now, I wish I could grab her by the shoulders, the idiot who that Christmas was so scared of becoming a mother. I want to grab the stupid coward, shove her against the wall, no matter how pregnant she is, and say, look around, for god's sake, stop and take a look around. Stop being scared and look at where you are.

I hate her, that me, so full and ungrateful. I despise her. I want her dead.

It was supposed to be an amazing year.

Giulia sends me a message in November 2020, the day after my third embryo transfer. I'm already resisting being a mother, going on a twenty-kilometre hike with some of my closest friends, to whom I've said nothing. I'm going on this hike, I tell myself, because I've tried the natural way for years and it hasn't worked, I've tried fertility treatment twice and it didn't work. This is the third and I can't let myself hope. The disappointment afterwards is too great. But that's my rational self talking. My real self, who never listens to anyone, only her own inner voice, says: it's going to work – it has to.

Giulia sends me a message: 'It's going to be an amazing year. Your novel's going to be huge and you're going to have your baby. I know it.' In the bathroom at the place we've stopped to eat after the hike, I sneak another look. Don't fall for it, I repeat to myself. Don't hope. But – not so much that day as in the impossible months that followed – I've learned that hope is like when you look at the sun for too long. First there's light, then the light becomes too much and burns your retinas: everything goes black. Hope is the spot that appears in your vision from having looked at the sun. It keeps getting bigger, chipping away at everything else until it takes over. I've learned that when hope grows too much, it becomes conviction. It might be associated with green but it's not green or even yellow. Hope is black, because it obscures you. One of the voices in me gets too loud and drowns out the others, saying: there's no way it won't work this time. You are going to have a baby in August. Sun, sea, they'll be a Leo, maybe have the same birthday as Elsa Morante, 18 August, but hopefully will be much happier. Or maybe they'll be born the same day as their father, 6 August. They'll inherit his calm and his cheerfulness. What will they get from me? I don't know, but I promise myself I'll be the kind of mother who smiles, her child's guiding light. That's what I want above all: to be my child's rock. The anxiety I've always struggled with – I'll stifle it for the child. I wouldn't want them to know who I really am.

Could I really do it?

Now, as I write, is it a lie to say that one of the reasons I put off deciding on having children for so long was the fear of not being able to show them my real self?

The fear of not being able to do my work. The fear of not knowing how to hide who I really am. Every reason I've had, all these years, for not bringing a child into the world – I curse it.

I'd always pictured a girl, before it happened. Then when it did, I was sure it was a boy. Instead, it was three girls. Three little girls who, in the twelve-week ultrasound, were happy inside me. One lying on her back with crossed legs seemed like Huck Finn staring up at the sky chewing on a blade of wheat. Another was sleeping all cosy and serene ('That one takes after you,' I said to Andrea). Another was thrashing about like a madwoman. 'That one takes after you,' Andrea said to me. 'She can't keep still, she's antsy. Like you.'

Like me.

Well, they are my daughters. And I'm their mother.

I don't know if I really want to write this book. I don't know if I know how. I read a few pages to Andrea but it's too much to ask of him. Andrea is a director and a screenwriter, there's nothing I send into the world without having him read it first. Andrea is intelligent, talented and rigorous. When he says something I write doesn't work, it doesn't work. And yet, when I read him a few pages of this, for the first time since we've been together he doesn't know what to say. It's too much to ask of him this time. He was awash in that river of blood, too.

And although Andrea never says he's hurting, never shows it, this time I can see that he's suffering. This is his story too. It's not only a mother's story. It's also a father's. It would be selfish to think of myself as the only protagonist of this pain.

I read him a few pages. I read them out loud and he listens and says: 'You do realise that if you do this book, it's going to be excruciating? When it comes out you're going to have to retell the story over and over for months.'

'So? What do I do? Give up? It doesn't make sense to write?' I ask.

He's making pasta sauce. Dark red.

'Hey,' I nudge. 'Answer me, please.'

'I think you should do it,' he says, almost imperceptibly. 'I think it's right.'

'But you can't help me to figure out what I'm writing.'

He shakes his head, he's sorry: no. 'I think you should do it,' he says. 'But do you have it in you to spend a year reliving everything that happened?'

I can't hold back the tears, but I hide them, because I always hate anyone to see me cry, and most of all I hate crying, and I want to tell him: when the book comes out everything will be different. I'm writing not with the hope but with the absurd conviction that the book will have a happy ending. I can't believe that it will end badly. I can't. Even now, after everything that happened.

But that's more magical thinking. An absurd conviction. And hope, as I have learned, can be violent.

I don't reply. I do what I always do: start joking around, talking nonsense. Dancing. Bugging him while he's cooking. I regret crying, even if only for a moment.

I never wanted to be like this.

I've always loved blood. The blood of cuts, knees scraped roller-skating in the courtyard, scratches from rocks where you jumped into the sea from some impossible spot; the blood of childhood pacts you believe in fiercely, the blood of syringes for medical tests. I always loved it because it made me feel brave.

I got my first period at fourteen, and I loved that my body dripped blood, though it always seemed like so little, and later, I loved having sex in menstrual blood, how it all seemed more fluid, more dangerous, more dynamic: sex seemed even better with all that blood.

But for the last five years I've hated it.

I always told myself I would never become this kind of woman – the kind who hates getting her period because it's a testament to her failure. I hated it when I finally decided to have a child, at nearly thirty-eight – 'Tsk

tsk tsk,' I can hear my sister and other women I know saying, 'Why did you wait so long?' and then others saying, 'Don't worry, you're young, you have plenty of time.' I hated it when I tried to get pregnant spontaneously, having sex whenever I felt like it, thinking that this was how children are conceived (that's how everyone else does it, right?), and it didn't work. When I started tracking my fertility window, going to the gynaecologist every month to monitor my cycle (turning sex into a chore, a bitter pill you're obligated to take at least every other day for a week), and it still didn't work. When both Andrea and I had taken every test in the world and there was nothing wrong with us, and therefore nothing that could be fixed. 'Unexplained infertility.' When I went through the process of assisted procreation, and by some cosmic joke, my first monitoring visit, at the beginning of March 2020, coincided with the first week of Covid lockdown, and a few weeks later at the Policlinico in Rome I had to have my retrieval done without anaesthesia because all the anaesthetists were busy with Covid patients (see, you deserved it). Then, I hated that blood.

I didn't want to become this kind of woman. I always told myself I never would.

What you become, of course, is your choice. What happens to you, not so much. To find out who you'll actually become, you have to wait for the future to happen. Only once the future has happened do you find out if you've let yourself down. If you're the very person you hoped not to become. That was me.

A woman who thinks of nothing but having a child. A woman who looks at pregnant women with envy. (You're writing, you have to be honest.) All right, I'll be honest. I look at them with hate.

And what if you're just talking to yourself? I wonder. For a book to be a book it can't speak only to you. It has to be for everyone. How can I tell if I'm just talking to myself?

A book is a serious thing. You can't write just to vent. You can't write just because it serves you.

I also deserved what happened because, as I'm searching for the courage to write all this, I think: Will it be a book? A good book?

I deserved it because, even now, instead of thinking about what happened, I'm thinking about writing. Even now, with three baby girls gone.

But I'm putting off the remembering part.

To write this book, I have to open doors that I never want to open again.

I'm afraid to look at those memories. Especially the happy ones. The happy ones, I'd rather never think of again.

('It's time to turn the page,' someone told me not long ago. Turn the page – even now it all comes back to books. 'You'll try again,' someone else wrote to me when I was in hospital and had just lost everything. If murder by telepathy were possible, the person who wrote me that message would have been dead on the spot.)

Summary: (remember, be honest.)

I always said I wanted five kids. I said this and believed it for as long as I can remember. I always told myself, but at the right time. I love big families.

At eighteen, I get pregnant. It's not for this book to say why, but I decide to have an abortion. At twenty, I get pregnant again. It's not for this book to say why that one didn't become my child either.

At thirty-four, I get together with Andrea. With him, the idea of having a child becomes real: a want. I try to talk him into it. He says yes, but 'later'. This 'later' never turns into 'now'. I can't put all the blame on him (I would if I could). At the time, I need support. I want a child badly, but I'm also terrified to have one. Theoretically I need a man to take me in his arms, look at me romantically and say: 'Let's make a baby.' Andrea, unromantically, requires convincing. I don't have the strength to convince him because I have to convince myself too. Moreover, Andrea has bright, dreamy eyes that, if he were a fictional character, would be inconsistent with his personality. Finally, after years of pressure, he grudgingly agrees. And at that point, I'm ready, but I stall: my third novel is about to come out. I'm afraid that a pregnancy would be bad for the book so I say: 'It's not the right time.'

It keeps not being the right time for a while, for me or for him. One night I look at him and say, 'If we don't do this now, we never will. You have to decide whether you want it. And if you don't, despite myself, I might have to leave you' (I was also terrified of becoming this kind of woman, but I did). I muster all my courage. He's not sure, but he makes an effort to summon his. We start trying.

As I said, having sex when we feel like it doesn't work. The various ovulation calculators that predict your fertile days don't work. Going alone to the gynaecologist every month to monitor my fertility window and having sex as if by prescription on what the fertility websites and apps (I downloaded four of them) indicate cutely as 'the right days' doesn't work. Every month, for seven to ten days, I conscript my partner to conjugal duty. He can't take it any more; imagine how I feel. Not only do I, like him, have to have sex when I have to and not when I want to (it's fun at first, but after a while I think both of us would rather be doing anything else on earth), but I also have to go up to Andrea sheepishly like, *you know what today is . . .* I ask him jokingly if he can try to remember the 'right days' too. At least we can be playful. But he never remembers. More than anything, it's humiliating. And regardless, it all comes to nothing. We decide to try fertility treatment.

We have no idea what we're getting ourselves into. Andrea goes ahead with it more for me than for us or for himself (another cliché I would have preferred to avoid . . .). So I do everything. Tests, calculations, monitoring, doctor visits, researching, learning, searching, finding. For his semen analysis, I take his specimen to the lab. I'm afraid that if I ask him for even the slightest effort, the slightest commitment, he'll say, that's enough, I don't want to do this any more.

For our first round of treatment we go to Policlinico Umberto I. Fertility treatment means a ton of tests, monitoring – at the hospital, in this case – a ton of medications – oral, vaginal – and injections. It means constant hormones and a 10 per cent reduction in quality of life (at the time it felt like 80 per cent, but I didn't know what else I had coming). It means retrieval at the right time, taking the man's semen (from jacking off in the hospital bathroom) and the woman's eggs (you get pumped with hormones then go in to get your follicles emptied). It's an operation performed under anaesthesia or sedation. Though not for me. It's March 2020, the beginning of the first lockdown, nobody knows anything for certain about Covid, and I'm terrified of going to the hospital and getting sick. It seems like the most absurd thing to do, going into a hospital. Masks aren't even mandatory yet. They give them to us inside, and you're not allowed to bring anyone with you. But there's more. There are no anaesthetists available because of the emergency. 'Do you want to skip this one and come back in a few months?' they ask. But I'm not the kind of person who, once I get something in my head, can set it aside. I do the retrieval 'raw', as they put it. 'You deserve to get pregnant after going through this,' a teary-eyed nurse says to me. And I think, damn it, why does everyone always associate maternity with sacrifice and pain? Maybe this is another reason I didn't deserve to get pregnant. Because I can't stand this figure of the suffering mother who immolates herself for her children and ceases to exist as a human being.

After retrieval, the woman's eggs and the man's sperm are combined in a lab. There are different techniques and levels of intervention, depending on your age. In March 2020, I'm already 40 and a half. They choose the highest-level procedure, in vitro fertilisation of the embryos – IVF – then wait to see which ones make it to day five and become blastocysts. Two survive. They transfer both, because there is no cryopreservation at Umberto I (which means blastocysts can't be stored for later use). More medication follows, and I'm convinced I'm pregnant (ignorance is bliss). Throughout this entire ordeal, before, after, countless times during the torment, I had to bite my tongue not to say to Andrea: I'm going through torture and all you had to do was jerk off in the bathroom. I wait fifteen never-ending days to find out whether, as they say, the embryos have implanted (I'm secretly terrified that both of them will and I swear and double-swear that if I get pregnant with twins I'll die, I'll kill myself, I'll throw myself off the balcony – another thing you'll be punished for – but the doctors assure me that won't happen, an assurance I'll later realise was meaningless). I wait these fifteen days feeling totally pregnant. Giulia, my only friend who knows what's going on, tells me: don't eat salami, don't eat spicy food, wash your produce with baking soda. We're certain I'm pregnant. I spend my time looking up every tiny indication of pregnancy on the internet. I say nothing to Andrea. I have no idea how, after everything happens, no longer having to wash my produce with baking soda will break my heart. Little things like that. They burrow into your brain, drive you crazy. On day fifteen I get my blood test with my beta-hCG levels (that's betas – stay with me, I've learned a lot). I go to the lab (alone), my heart bursting. Now I hate that street from my house to the lab. When I pass it, I don't want to cry. I want to blow it up. At the time, though, all I care about is whether this baby exists. While I'm in a work meeting online, while the world is in lockdown, I get the email with the lab results. Zero. Nothing. I have to go on with the meeting. I remember nothing about it. It ends. I log off. I tell Andrea, 'I'm not pregnant.' 'What do you mean you're not pregnant?' he asks in disbelief. But I don't cry with him. I cry with my gynaecologist, Dr S, and most of all with Giulia. This collapsing world is something I can share only with her. But I can't see her. We're stuck home. I cry over the phone. I suspect Andrea isn't as distraught as I am. Actually, I know he isn't. I suspect Andrea doesn't even mind. I hate him.

I don't tell anyone anything. Not even the people closest to me. The truest friends I've got.

This round of IVF, in March, is my last before everything shuts down. Months follow where, confined to my house like everyone else, I go crazy. I have to wait for the procedures to start up again, but the clock is ticking and I realise too late just how behind I am. The doctors tell me that my chances of getting pregnant, even with IVF, at my age, are less than 15–20 per cent. According to some, as low as ten.

As soon as regular medical protocols can resume, on 20 April, I start again. In the meantime, everything has changed. I search high and low – on my own, Andrea doesn't search for anything – and find an affiliated clinic in another city, let's call it Y. They have an office in Rome, but retrieval and transfer are done in Y. After speaking with the secretary at the clinic, I assure Andrea that his only obligation is to come with me to Y for the retrieval. I research everything on my own, I go to all the appointments on my own, I do everything on my own.

I don't write this to fault Andrea; this is a summary of events. I resume the endless, expensive hormone treatments. The endless, expensive monitoring. The endless, expensive blood tests. I wake up at dawn with a headache I can't shake and go to the Rome office of the gynaecologist from Y for my appointment. I wait hours and hours, first to have my blood taken at the clinic-affiliated lab, then for monitoring at the gynaecologist's. I stand in line outside the lab, at seven in the morning, in the cold. Because of Covid, waiting inside isn't allowed. I wait on the stairs outside the office, standing or sitting on the steps. Because of Covid, no more than four people are allowed inside at the same time. There are lots of us. We share our experiences. I'm one of the oldest. I feel old. And I'm very tired.

I return home and I'm tense, furious at Andrea for not having to deal with any of this – but I don't say so, because I'm afraid he'll respond that I should stop. I'm furious at Andrea for not seeming to see anything I'm going through.

I do everything. The medications, the tests, the injections. I show signs of hyperstimulation. We can do the retrieval, but not the transfer, I'm told. It'll be at least a couple of months before we can try again. Once my period comes back, I have to start taking the pill, and then I can expect to start another cycle. The meaning of *expecting* is turned on its head. I'm not pregnant, I'm not expecting a child. I'm expecting something to happen that only has a 10 per cent chance of success. When they tell me I can't do the transfer immediately after the retrieval, but have to wait months – all while you're very old to have a child, you're getting even older – I want to go home and flip the table over. Take a hatchet to the sofa. Just be in Andrea's arms. Instead, I take the pill to 'reset' my ovaries.

My period is supposed to come in June. It doesn't come in June, nor in July. A summer where all I do is wait. I hate the word 'wait'. I always have and now even more. In June, Andrea takes a long and difficult directing job. From that point on, he disappears. The job sucks up I don't even know how many hours of his day. When he gets home, he's cranky and tired. I lose touch with him completely and talk only to Giulia. Then Giulia leaves for vacation. I leave town too, first to a country house in Tuscany, without Andrea, and then to Sperlonga, near Circeo, from where, at that moment, I can't imagine that less than a year later I'll be racing down the Pontina in the middle of the night hoping not to bleed to death. In that August 2020, I spend a month in Sperlonga with four of my dearest friends. Sometimes Andrea joins us for the weekend. I don't say anything to my four dear friends. They have no idea.

I take hormones, the pill, medications. My period finally comes on 11 August. I have to start treatment to prepare my ovaries and my uterine lining for implantation. Starting on 11 August, I have to start monitoring to determine when I can do the transfer in Y. Of course, during the August holidays in Sperlonga, a beach town where I would have loved to lose myself in the joy of expecting, no ultrasound labs are open. But if I don't do this monitoring now, I'll have to wait another menstrual cycle. More waiting is out of the question.

I spend the day I get my period calling every ultrasound centre in the vicinity. I call, I ask, finally I beg. The gynaecologist at the clinic in Y tells me to forget it and try during my next cycle. For the second time, they say, Do you want to skip this round? No, I don't and I can't. On the beach, I spend the whole day making calls. I ask Andrea, who happens to be there and not working because it's Assumption, 'Will you help me?' He doesn't help, he reads the latest Stephen King.

It doesn't even anger me. I can't spare the energy. I have to stay focused. As the sun starts to set, he finishes his book and I find an ultrasound technician in Terracina, thirty or forty minutes away. I don't know him, he was on holiday, but I begged. I'm good at pleading with doctors.

On 18 August at 8 a.m. I have my first monitoring appointment. Andrea doesn't come. He's tired. He has to go back to the shoot in Rome. I come up with some excuse to explain to my friends why, four times, on alternate days, I wake up at dawn to go all the way to Terracina. I'm a good liar. I've always been a good liar. Many times in my life I've wondered how people believe the bullshit I come up with. Maybe they don't want to know the truth; maybe I actually have a knack for it. I'm not a habitual liar, though. I tell lies, even big ones, only when it's a matter of keeping that dam inside me closed, and I don't want to look, don't want to share. I've done it for as long as I can remember.

I load up on hormones, injections, suppositories, progesterone pills. My phone has a whole series of alarms: as someone who is chaos personified, I can't risk getting anything wrong. I take 400 mg of folic acid, 5 mg of Prednisone, 0.3 ml injections of Fraxiparine, 2 mg Progynova tablets (morning, noon and night), 25 mg liquid Prolutex (2 injections a day), 50 mg Estraderm patches (2 every 48 hours). Ten alarms. I'm with my friends all day. Every time an alarm goes off, they're there. Sometimes I remember to take the medication before it rings; other times, very often, it rings in front of them. 'Why do you have an alarm at two in the afternoon?' I laugh. 'Just a mistake,' I reply. 'Why is your alarm going off at midnight?' We laugh because it's quirky, I've always been quirky, and a few extra quirks here or there don't make much of a difference. But one day Emilio, as we're having dinner and my alarm goes off at midnight, innocently asks, 'What are all these alarms about?' I'm constantly self-conscious, inserting suppositories in the changing room at the beach club, giving myself injections in restaurant bathrooms. Sometimes I have to prepare a solution, adding water to powdered medicine. It's not easy in a café bathroom, they're not clean, and I'm terrified of messing up. But what else can I do. Emilio expects an entertaining response. I don't have an excuse prepared – I'm not sure why, since I have excuses and fabrications for everything else – and I mutter, 'it's a gynecological treatment,' guaranteeing he won't press for more. Why don't I make something up?

I don't because one day I hope to be able to say, actually, this is why I had all those alarms. I want to be at least minimally honest, for once. I don't want to lie. I just want to keep this a secret for as long as possible.

I take the medications. I do the injections. I go for monitoring. I send the reports to the doctor at the Y clinic. At the end of all this, I get the green light. On 31 August I'm to go to Y for the transfer. Naturally, Andrea doesn't come. I have three blastocysts. They ask if I want to transfer one or two. They recommend one, because a twin pregnancy is much higher risk. The Y clinic does cryopreservation. If I choose to transfer one, the remaining two can be used later. I can try again, if it doesn't work this time.

I wish I could talk to Andrea but he hasn't been present, hasn't done any reading about it, hasn't been consumed by all this since October 2019, when I had my first consultation for assisted reproduction at the Policlinico. He says, 'OK, let's do whatever they say.'

This instantly angers me. It's no more or less serious than the other times, but this time I can't contain myself. I'm angry like never before (usually I don't get angry, not because I don't hate him but because I need him on my side and anger's not to my advantage; I become a strategist, a mathematician, calculating in a way I've never been). This time, yes. I'm angry for real. I throw his total absence in his face. Only by text, though. Then I stop – I have to stay focused. I arrange with the clinic for a single transfer as they recommend.

I get back to Rome on 30 August, late afternoon, driving with my dear friends who have no idea what's going on. I told them I had to go to Y the next day for some kind of medical appointment. I made up a lie I don't even remember now, and they believed it.

The next day I take the train to Y at dawn. It feels like winter came overnight, it's insanely cold. There's Covid. What point of lockdown are we at? I don't remember. It's the period after mid-August when cases are on the rise again. In Y, there's not a coffee bar or restaurant where you can sit down. Only take-out. I don't want to eat, I just want to sit. I'm cold, it's windy and rainy. I take the tram to the clinic. There's Covid. I can't go inside until it's my turn. I wait outside in the cold. All the other women are with their partners and husbands. I try not to think about that. I have to stay focused. The transfer is extremely painful – I have cervical stenosis, so even this procedure which isn't supposed to hurt is painful for me. As they're working on me they say, 'Look at the blastocyst racing into your body, it's so exciting!' To me it's not exciting whatsoever. I don't want to look. I don't want to hope. This is just a mechanical procedure. I'm not excited.

I get back on the tram, worn out, and I have this thing inside me that I don't want to think about in any way except as a 'thing'. I get to the station an hour before the train back to Rome. There's Covid and it's cold. Everything is prohibited. I sit down on the ground, on a curb next to the street. And I wait. Theoretically even this is prohibited.

Pause.

For the last three years up to now, this chilly 31 August, I've been working on my new novel. I never thought there was a connection between the story of a woman trapped in a house with two little girls she no longer wants and everything I've been doing to get pregnant. I sincerely never thought there was. And sincerely there isn't. That summer of 2020 in Sperlonga, I come up with a title for the novel and the cover. The book will come out in January 2021. I've never thought of books as children, much less now. The mere idea repulses me. Books are not children at all. But it's around books that my life has always revolved. And so I'm torn between these two waits. Waiting for the novel to come out, all the work of writing, rewriting, editing, coming up with a title, the cover design, organising the launch, and this other wait. The trulyheart-pounding hope of getting pregnant. The truly heart-pounding hope that the book will be wonderful, well-received, celebrated.

This is a summary, but I have to make one point. I have to do it, for the sake of honesty. I didn't have a child sooner, when I still had time, because I wouldn't have been able to work the way I do – or rather, I was terrified I wouldn't be able to – if I had a child. There is no one who can help you be a woman with ambitions and a woman who wants to be a mother at the same time. The first time I got pregnant, no matter what I tell myself, I had an abortion because I wanted to be a writer. The second time, too.

The days of waiting begin again. In the meantime, we edit the book, we organise the launch, we decide on the title and the cover, and I am split in two. One part who works, and one who obsessively looks up pregnancy sites.

I have a wedding coming up in Procida. Andrea will meet me there, later, because he has to work. The days go by. I take a home pregnancy test. I don't say anything to the gynaecologist at the clinic in Y and I don't say anything to Andrea. Only Giulia. I send her a photo of the test strip. 'Does that look positive to you?' I ask (it's not a serious test, just one of those little papers that look like a litmus strip and you can't tell if the pink line is really there or you're imagining it). Giulia replies, 'Yes! You're pregnant! Yes!' I don't know if I see it, if the photo is bad, but then the day for the blood test comes and I have to leave for Procida. I haven't got the results yet. On the ferry, surrounded by friends and acquaintances who have no idea what's going on, I get an email. This time, instead of the word 'negative' there's beta and the number 76. I look it up and find out that's not very high, but the gynaecologist at the Y clinic and Giulia and I each say yes, it's happening. I don't say anything to Andrea, but I'm bursting.

I don't say anything when he arrives – he knew I was expecting my results, he asked me for updates several times, but not with much confidence – and I don't say anything until we're back at the hotel that night. I don't know how he was able to wait all that time.

I think he had an inkling, otherwise I would have told him it was a no. I don't know how he was able to respect my 'wait, I'll tell you later'. I'm half surprised, half indignant. He doesn't give a shit, I keep thinking. And then I say to myself: you can't give a shit whether he gives a shit.

I tell him the results that night, and I also tell him that we have to wait, because the beta level is very low. It could be a faint positive, something that won't have time to exist and will end. I say this, but I don't think it. I'm trying not to explode with joy. He smiles. 'Say something, are you happy?' I ask. If he were a character in a novel, it wouldn't be in his character to say much. I can ask all I want.

But at the wedding the next day, he sticks close.

After, with some friends, we go for a swim in that deep dark-blue Procida sea. It's incredible. I say to the little thing inside me: look, this is the sea.

Two days later, on the train back, I can feel that something is gone. I don't know if it's a physical sensation, or mental, or just a coincidence. On the ferry and then on the train, with my friends, I talk about how hot it was, or how good the pasta with clams was, the guests I liked and didn't like, and I listen to them talk about how gorgeous the bride's dress was and who they liked and didn't like, but in reality I only feel one thing: it's all over. That night I take another home test. The line is almost invisible. The next day I take another beta test. They've gone down. They'll keep going down until they disappear. If only I could disappear too.

All over again.

You wait for your period.

Tests, medications, monitoring, the works. All over again.

The months go by.

My novel's publication day approaches.

We figured out the title. We figured out the cover.

I love them both: the title, the cover.

Now, as I write, I'm trying to look at those months. I don't see anything. I don't remember anything. Now, as I write, I stop and check the photos on my phone. They'll be able to tell me something about what I did while I was waiting for my life to finally happen; on these two fronts that will never again be separate. I try to remember doing the testing, monitoring, and all the rest. And other things, I'm sure.

I look at the photos. They tell me nothing.

Andrea works all the time, all day. I get ready for the book launch and I wait. For my novel to come out. For my child to exist.

I'm excited, hopeful, thrilled, demoralised, disappointed, hopeful, thrilled, tired, stuffed with hormones, drugs, injections, excited, hopeful, thrilled, desperate; a liar.

In November, I go back to Y for the transfer. Right before, they call me to ask how many 'blasts' I want transferred (that's what they call them, like trying to make it into something fun, blasts instead of blastocytes, US is short for ultrasound; I try to keep up with the lingo) of the two I have left. I want to do both, since I'm about to turn forty-one and have already gone through two failed cycles. But they've terrified me with the possibility of a twin pregnancy, and I don't know if I could handle that. I ask for advice. One of the Y clinic gynaecologists tells me, 'It's your decision, but I understand if you want to try with two. No risk, no reward,' he says. 'Of course, that's just my personal view.' I talk to Andrea in the scant time we're together. We fought a lot during those months. I fought with him brazenly. Without the least concern that he might say I've had enough, let's stop trying. We fought so much one night that for the first time in six years I told him, don't come home tonight. He said: 'OK, let's do two.'

I go back to Y. Again, on my own.

But this time it's not in a late-August wind that chills my bones. This time, as long as I wear a mask, I can sit in the waiting room. And as I wait to be called in, the editor-in-chief calls, from the publishing house that's putting out my novel in January. We're preparing the final proofs to send to the printer, she says. She asks if I have time to review a few last queries. Instinctively I start to say to call back later. But then I realise I don't want her to. In the solitude of this pink-walled waiting room, I pull out my headphones, open up my computer, and murmur, 'I'm in the waiting room at the doctor's, but we can get started.' She replies that it can wait, there's no rush. But I want to work on my book. I don't want to just wait here, alone and scared. It's not like me to sit alone and scared. I'll never forget that phone call. Now, as I write, I have the call burned into my brain. Her putting to me her final questions, me responding. And not only does my time in this room go by more quickly, it's also nice. I'm doing something, and being active is what I know. I'm doing something for the book and I'm doing something for someone who might be born to me. I have no idea how long I've been in that waiting room. We finish everything. Just after, they call me in. 'Are you ready?' I'm ready. You have no idea how long I've been ready.

Stop.

Among other things, my novel that's coming out is the story of a mother who no longer knows if she wants to be a mother. A mother who is unbearably lonely, who spends all her time cooped up at home with two young daughters without being able to do anything else. Sometimes, she hates those little girls.

When I wrote it, I was afraid it was inauthentic. I wasn't a mother. I had no idea that once it came out, at every reading, someone would ask: do you have children? Each time I replied with a different attitude.

When one of the editors at the publishing house read it for the first time, they said, 'I don't know how you were able to write about motherhood without having children. Either you have them and you've kept it from me' – she laughed – 'or you don't want them with every fibre of your being' – and she laughed again. I laughed too – to think of all the times I laughed even though I was breaking inside, through these months, this year – it's been almost a year – that I promoted the book. I laughed and said, I think, 'no, of course, I don't want them.'

Meanwhile, not long before my birthday – 20 November – I told my friend Ada. We were hanging out one evening, and at some point, I don't remember how, it just came out. I told her everything I had gone through up to that point. She was upset, and I cried. 'Why didn't you tell me before? I'm sorry I wasn't there for you.' I couldn't tell anyone anything. But now I had done it. From now on, she knows.

Every time I tell someone – at the moment, very few people know: me, Andrea, Giulia, and now Ada – it feels like I lose a little strength. Part of the reserve behind my dam.

I hate going to the therapist – I never do, through this whole story, although everyone recommends it: friends, doctors, the hospital. I hate going to the therapist and I always have, it makes me feel like a sick person. As soon as I sit down in front of a therapist, I mistrust them. I get nervous. I never thought I was one of those 'if you don't say it, it doesn't exist' people. I found out I am. I don't want to bring up things that make me feel bad. No past. No present. No future. Up to now, I haven't told anyone what I was going through, not because it would be too painful – the prevailing, idiotic sentiment is still hope – but because of the other kind of magical thinking: if you speak it, it won't come true. I obsessively fantasised – all the time, and even now – about the moment I could call a friend and say: guess what, it finally happened. The kind of call I've received many times in my almost forty-two years on earth. 'Toni? I have news,' and the woman's voice on the other end is effervescent, it tells me everything. She doesn't even have to say it because I already know. 'I have news. I'm pregnant!' That call. That one. How long I've fantasised about being the one to make that phone call.

*

Every time I tell someone else what I'm trying to do, it feels like I lose a little strength. But this time, when I tell Ada, it's because I think it's going to happen. That soon I'll be making that phone call. And it's nice to have someone waiting with you for that moment.

On the day of my transfer at the clinic in Y, 25 November, I invite a friend and his partner over for dinner (in flagrant disregard of the latest curfew – we're degenerates). My friend is turning forty. He's going through a rough time. Andrea and I want to give him a little relief. I'm there with my friend but I'm also somewhere else entirely.

I just got home from Y. If there's something inside me, this is how I'm caring for it. With this dinner.

The next day I go on that twenty-kilometre hike up Monte Mario. My friend Giulia tells me, 'Be careful – walking is fine, but don't wear yourself out.' I didn't intend to go all the way up the mountain, it just happened that way. I hiked all twenty kilometres, blasé, cocky, I don't even know why. Because I'm so naively trusting? In what? In whom? Or because I'm not a good mother who knows how to protect her children? Because I never grew up and my life still revolves around a challenge (and yet who exactly am I challenging now)? I did a lot of things – good, bad, stupid – in my youth, and I haven't changed. A little voice will tell me: this is dangerous! Or: you can't do that! I pretend to think it over, then respond: what's the big deal, of course I can.

'Good morning, Doctor. I took another beta test yesterday and it's 6682 (I transferred two blastocysts, hopefully one has attached . . .). The clinic says to continue my usual treatment and take another beta test in 5–7 days. What do you think?'

The phone containing the first messages where my beta levels are finally positive, a very high number, something like 700 – is lost. There's no trace of those messages.

There's no trace of when I secretly took those pregnancy tests, which I hid from everyone except Giulia, or of when I sent my first positive result to Giulia, to the Y clinic doctor, and Dr S. in Rome.

There's a gap in the messages, which jump from the last time everything failed to 15 December when I write that message to my gynaecologist in Rome – my real gynaecologist, who becomes like a father and a doctor to me, with the plusses and minuses of both a father and a doctor. He doesn't answer my text. Because he calls. He calls me, spontaneously, happy because he's been with me all these years of trying. He's excited, and the happiness in his voice is contagious.

(Are you sure you can bear to read those messages? Are you sure you can do it, open the file of horror where you keep all the tests, the scans, the reports detailing everything that happened? Are you sure you can throw open that door? Right now, as I write, Andrea is next to me. He's working. I didn't tell him I'm still writing this book. I want to show him these pages more than anything, but I've fallen back into silence.)

On the days when my beta levels are rising, they double, quadruple (I could go on the medical lab's website and download my first beta test and get the exact number, can I handle it? No, which is why I wrote 'something like 700' so I didn't have to look back at the report. But either you have the courage to write this book or you don't. And so, fine, I let a day or two go by, go to the lab results page, and click to download. I look: beta-hCG: 8 December: 258, 10 December: 764, 14 December: 6682. A voice tells me, stop, stop with this book, what's the point of all this suffering, but I can't stop, I immediately delete all the reports, I open the Downloads folder, delete, delete, delete). The days when my beta levels are rising, Andrea is on a film shoot. If it's possible, he's around even less than before. I'm overjoyed by these levels, but terrified too. I know I transferred two embryos. I know that at the Y clinic they explained to me in every way possible that a multiple pregnancy would be very dangerous. I also know for certain that I don't want twins. I can't even imagine twins (see, you deserved it). And so, my betas skyrocketing, it's December, it's cold, I'm nauseous, and I don't want to say anything to Andrea because I'm afraid he'll get spooked. I keep my doubts (is it twins?) to myself.

Or not quite. I tell Giulia about them. I tell her again and again. She laughs as if it's absurd. 'No, of course it's not,' she says, and on the phone we compare her beta levels during her first and second pregnancies at her first, second, and third tests. Giulia is patient – with me; she isn't usually, but through all these months she is. I've given her this enormous responsibility of being my go-to person through the whole story, and she has accepted it. It's never Andrea I go to with my worries, my fears about work – I'm always terrified he'll say, well if you're scared, it's never going to happen. Instead I tell Giulia about my nightmares – the book, twins – and she's the one I send my photos and screenshots and messages to. She's there through all of it.

The doubt is gut-wrenching. How would I be able to work with twins? My parents live far away, Andrea's mother is always busy. We don't have the money for a nanny. When Andrea is prepping a movie or on set he's almost never around. How would we manage with two? What would become of my work – that is, of me?

I must be completely honest: work is my greatest concern. Some might be able to understand this. And I have another: travelling. I love to travel. It's the thing I love most besides writing. How would I be able to keep travelling with twins? Or even with one? (See, with these awful, selfish thoughts, you got what you deserved.)

Now, in November 2021, almost a year after, the empty-me wants to crucify the mother-me from the year before. Why can't you see that you're the luckiest woman in the world, Antonella? Or Toni, as people call myself. For god's sake, she says (her voice shaky, the voice of the weak, useless present-me), you should damn well be enjoying every minute of this. Because when it's over, you'll have to fight to hold on to your sanity like never before. Sure, there have been other times you thought you were losing it. But never a despair like this.

On the days I have no record of because I lost my phone, I start feeling nauseous. But I don't feel tired; I never feel tired during the pregnancy. I don't feel tired, but I do feel scared. And then, I lose my phone. And I spend that day – and there's no trace of Andrea, he's just a hazy name, like someone you haven't seen for decades and can't clearly recall – I spend that day

going back and forth, walking everywhere – I can't
travel by scooter after the transfer, and by the time
all this is over, I'll have spent hundreds of euros on
taxis, because the scooter has betrayed me just like
everything else, now I can use it as much as I want
and it has become a symbol of everything I've lost,
and I never want to see it again – I walk everywhere
because I have to get a new phone and my betas are
very high and I keep texting Giulia what if it's twins,
and Giulia says let's hope not, and I say let's hope not,
then she says, you could have twins, and I say no, not
twins, it'd be impossible, you're nuts, and I imagine
scenarios – the kind that led me to wait too long to
start trying for a baby, scenarios as specific images:
my work as a building constructed brick by brick, year
after year, suddenly imploding and turning to dust,
me stuck at home all day while others win Nobels,
interstellar prizes and go to the moon; I imagine these
scenarios of destruction, sitting on the steps outside
my building, it's December, it's cold, late afternoon,
everything is dark, Andrea hasn't reacted to the news
that the embryo has implanted (it's too soon to say
'I'm pregnant' – in fact, it's a sentence I will never say,
I never make it there), I'm sitting on the steps outside
feeling desperate, I tell my friend if it's twins I'm out,
I'll just leave, and she replies, with a laugh: 'You can't
run away, where would you go? Whether it's one or
two they're inside you.'

And that's when it hits me (I had tremendous
moments of realisation, followed by awful moments of
non-acceptance, followed by moments of incredible joy
and fullness, but I never sat with a single moment that
stayed the same, I never managed to), that's when it
hits me and for the first time I see this one or these two

inside me, the poor things bouncing around all day, to and from the Apple store, up and down my sixth-story walk-up, with this dumb mother who wanted them so desperately and now is scared of them. It hits me and I say to myself: I can't run away. And for the first time in my life the phrase 'I can't run away' is a wonderful surprise. Not only can I not run away, but I don't want to. Wherever I go, so do they. They're always with me. On those steps, in the dark and the cold, it's a stunning discovery.

I can't run away. More importantly, I don't want to.

(In the meantime, I keep taking the medication and giving myself the injections necessary through the first trimester of pregnancy; I keep the alarms I've been using for months, for these injections and others. Once I don't need them any more, I turn them off in tears, not yet having the heart to delete them, the exact times and names of drugs to be swallowed or injected. Until one day, I'll take a deep breath and delete them all. It'll be an act of repression and I won't hesitate an instant before deleting, I'll delete without giving my brain the time to realise, remember, cry, I'll delete everything and then turn to Andrea, who doesn't see any of it, and say: 'Do you know why sometimes it's cold and sometimes it's super hot?' 'No,' he'll say, as if playing along with a five-year-old girl. 'I do: because there are seasons. Another case solved by Inspector Antonio' (that's me). And he'll smile and say, 'You're such a dork.' And I'll be a perfect Inspector Antonio, in fine form.)

'Good morning, doctor,' I text the Y clinic gynaecologist who oversaw my artificial insemination. 'I'm sending you my beta levels. Are they normal or a little high?'

Her reply: 'Let's wait for the first ultrasound to see if it's one or two ;).' What is she thinking with this wink emoji? Wasn't she the one who told me if two implanted it would be tragic? Why the hell is she winking at me?

Me: 'Could it really be twins?'

Her: 'We'll see at the ultrasound. My recommendation was to only transfer one.'

So why is she winking? Is it funny that I screwed up? Should I remind her that the other doctor there approved transferring two?

I don't have the message any more, I'm quoting from memory. It might not be exact, but that's the gist. I can still see the wink emoji: it's branded into my brain. I tell Giulia and Giulia says, 'What a bitch. Why don't you tell her off?' But I, throughout this entire thing, will never tell anyone off.

I won't have the will, the courage, the strength. Sometimes it'll be because I'm too happy to care about the indignities, sometimes because I'm too despondent to care about the offenses, sometimes because I'm at the doctors' mercy and my life or that of my daughters depends on them, sometimes because I'm obliterated, paralysed by too much joy or too much pain, sometimes because I want to avoid getting upset while I'm pregnant. I'm afraid of losing it. Losing him, her, them.

Now, as I write, my hate gleams like granite. I want to slit the throats, one by one, of every person who made this whole thing even more unbearable. I'm merciless.

(When all this is over, at first the people who know will be afraid to talk about children. Or when someone who doesn't know brings up children or pregnancy, those who do know will glance at me with concern. Andrea will try to keep me from movies with pregnancies and babies, or anything that might remind me of children. But I'll say no, please, talk, show, tell, I have to hear, see, feel. It doesn't hurt, I'll say. It's my personal shock therapy. My private rejection of what happened. I don't know if this is good or bad; I feel like it's good for others because they can say what they want. I feel like it's good for me because I can't live like this. Meanwhile, it all hurts. And in time everyone else seems to forget what happened because I never talk about it. That hurts even worse. To have no one asking me how I am, if I need to talk. I know they think they're being considerate: they don't broach the subject because they don't want to make me sad. They don't see that Toni, the one who's always fooling around, laughing, making light of things, even cracking jokes about what happened, is going around with a black hole inside.

They don't know because I don't let them know. It's part of my reserve. Yet if you don't show your suffering, how can people stand by you?

There's a caveat. Sometimes when you share your suffering, people abandon you. And rather than risk that kind of disappointment, I keep quiet. Or laugh.)

Andrea isn't insensitive though he may come across that way from what I'm writing. Andrea doesn't get emotional, or excited, but he brings me a flower. Or he cooks one of my favourite dishes. Or he's there, maybe in silence, but there, for all my ups and downs, on all my journeys into horror. Or not all, but most; after a certain point there are so many that I don't even tell him. Sometimes his presence makes no difference. Other times it does.

Andrea is there as much as he can be, in his own way, but in these months he's never around. Still, this battle is his too, and he's fighting it the best he can. But I don't know anything about it.

I don't eat jarred olives any more. They turn my stomach.

I don't drink coffee.

I don't eat prawns.

I don't eat any kind of food with dressing, it also turns my stomach.

I've always hated pizza. Now I eat nothing else. I want pizza all the time. I love it.

All the flavours I used to love send me to the toilet to throw up. After a while, I can't even stand wine or beer.

My biggest struggle is with cigarettes. I didn't ask the gynaecologist, because I didn't want to hear him say no. Another reason I don't deserve to be a mother:

I still smoke a few cigarettes a day. It used to be a full pack, so it's an improvement. But Toni, just think, how many times you've heard women say, I quit as soon as I found out I was pregnant.

Whereas I don't quit. I struggle like crazy but I can't get down to fewer than two or three.

The little girls I have in here forgive me. Mamma, they say, you are who you are. Or no, maybe these girls hate me. Mamma, they tell me, you're the worst mother in the world. Selfish. Or they blow me off. They loaf about all day, lying back chewing on a blade of grass and looking up at the sky, or dancing, or curled up for a nap. I don't know.

I don't even know that they're triplets.

Meanwhile, I can barely eat any more. I'm almost happy when I have to run off to vomit. The nausea is constant, so I'm happy to throw up. My only relief is Schweppes. I drink gallons of Schweppes but almost no alcohol, and I'm worried that my friends will notice this abrupt change of habits and suspect something. It worries me, though part of me wants them to.

How often in life have I wished that someone would see through my biggest lies.

Still nobody says anything, and my belly starts to grow because there's more than one baby inside me even if I don't know it yet, and my breasts swell. 'Look at these tits,' I say to Andrea. 'Aren't you happy?' and he laughs. Of course he's happy, and so am I, that finally I have these big tits to enjoy.

Nobody says a word. After a while, whenever I go to visit Emilio, one of the friends I went to Sperlonga with, one of my very closest, he tells me, 'I got your Schweppes,' with a smile, the same way he used to say, 'I got your beer.' How I loved that Schweppes. Just seeing it brought me bliss. I loved my friends so much, even if they didn't know anything. Even though I hadn't told them.

Dr. S, the gynaecologist in Rome who's like a father and a doctor to me, takes good care of me. He has me come in right away for an ultrasound when I tell him my high beta levels. He says that most likely only the yolk sac will be visible, but 'at least we'll be able to see if it's one or two'. That's it. It's early. But he knows how long I've been waiting for this moment. He says, 'Normally I would wait to do an ultrasound, but if you want to have one now, we'll do it.'

We do it.

Later, I will hate ultrasounds. Now, in that December 2020, I love them.

This isn't easy to write.

It's almost Christmas, and Andrea and I go to Dr S. It's the first time in all these years that Andrea has come with me to anything related to our 'trying' for a baby (I hate all these expressions). It's late afternoon. In Prati, it's already dark. 'What if it's nothing?' I said to Giulia. 'What if it's nothing?' I say to Andrea. I don't tell Andrea about all the time I spend on the internet researching pregnancy. The apps that tell you what the foetus looks like and what it's doing at every stage of pregnancy. The forums that tell you everything that can go wrong ('everything,' though I almost laugh at writing 'everything,' because none of them remotely approximated what I would go through). I'm terrified of having an ectopic pregnancy. I convince myself that

I do, for no reason. There's that magical-thinking voice inside me saying, it's impossible that something so wonderful, so monumental, could be happening to you.

Giulia told me, 'Relax!' Andrea tells me, 'Relax!'

Dr. S has me lie back on the exam table as I have a million times before to monitor my ovulation. There's a shadowy spot in my uterus. He smiles. 'That's the yolk sac.' I say, 'What does that mean?' He replies, 'It's too soon to see the embryo. But you are pregnant. There's only one sac. It's not twins. It's just one.' I say: 'Is it OK?' He smiles again and says I can get dressed. 'You're pregnant, Antonella. You're very pregnant. Don't be scared. Remember, pregnancy is not an illness.'

You're very pregnant.

Pregnancy is not an illness.

All the times these statements would come back into my head. But this isn't the moment for reflection. It's the moment when Andrea is holding my hand. I can't believe it's really happening.

We go home with the ultrasound picture of that little shadow: the yolk sac. I'm sure that shadow contains everything that's going to happen to us from this moment on. It's too big to really comprehend when you're living it.

A few days later, I have to take notes during a work call and I write them on the back of the ultrasound envelope because it's the only paper within reach. When I realise, I tell Andrea, laughing. I think of all the parents who keep every tiny thing related to their pregnancy as a sacred relic. In these months, I will save everything too. But distractedly jotting down notes on the envelope containing my first ultrasound makes me feel like a real mother. It's such a tender thing. I say so to Andrea. I laugh, he laughs. Then he leaves to go on set. Before he leaves, I ask, 'Are you happy, or are you worried?' If Andrea were a fictional character, he wouldn't be one for teary-eyed hugs. I don't know how he feels. I think he's confused. I think right now he is pushing his thoughts away. It's too soon. Anything could happen. Whether he does this because thinking would make him too happy or too scared, I don't know. I'm inclined to think the latter. But I couldn't care less right now. I. Am. Pregnant. Very pregnant.

'It's one! It's one! It's one!' I shout over the phone to Giulia. She laughs. 'Yes!' she exclaims. 'You're pregnant, you're pregnant!'

'This is the first time in my life,' I tell Andrea, 'that I'm happy about a positive test. The other two times, I knew I had to get an abortion. Those positives were horrible. Unspeakable. This is the first time it makes me happy.' I say this, my voice shaking, but if Andrea were in a novel, it wouldn't be in his character to get emotional now, and give me a hug.

Women who just can't seem to get pregnant. Those poor women. Friends, relatives, women in the forums. I look down on them. I don't feel lucky. I feel superior. Me, I am better. No one knows I'm pregnant. I dispense advice to those who aren't the way a queen tosses crumbs to her subjects.

When we get home, I ask Andrea to watch *The Neverending Story* with me. I loved it when I was a kid. I haven't seen it in decades.

I spend half the movie trying not to cry. And it's not because I'm pregnant (I never get that either, that thing that happens to other pregnant women who cry at nothing, who are moved just seeing a baby; I've never been a kid person and apparently I never will be). It's an intense, poignant movie, so full of imagination. Maybe even better now than when it came out.

I'm struck by the young protagonist's line just before the end.

'Why is it so dark?' Bastian asks the Empress after saving Fantasia, and everything is so dark and murky that it seems as if our heroes have lost.

'In the beginning, it is always dark,' the Empress replies.

I still love you, *Neverending Story*. This darkness that is a beginning, it feels like it's talking about me.

Immediately I write to my editor to ask if we have time before the book goes to print to add a line from this movie to the epigraphs.

We have time. We add it. 'But I can't! I have to keep my feet on the ground!' Bastian cries out tearfully, kept from dreaming by a reality he doesn't want, nor does my protagonist, and neither do I.

In this wholly dark world where everything is beginning for me, my book goes to print. It's a darkness full of warmth.

It's coming out on 14 January. And we – myself and those inside me (I don't know yet that we're all girls) – really are all here. Waiting, expecting for this novel that's on the way.

I'd wanted it so badly. I'd worked for it so hard. For years, whatever state I found myself in, whether dying of sadness and anxiousness or dying of happiness, with my head pulling me somewhere else, I had to stay the course. I wanted to stay the course.

When I was trying the natural way, I did the calculations with Giulia: 'If I get pregnant now and the novel comes out X month, how will I manage?' And after I started fertility treatment: 'if it works and I have a baby in X month, how I will I manage with the book?' Giulia answered the millions of paranoid messages I sent her from my hair salon in Piazza Vittorio; for some reason the moment I walked in there I'd start making these calculations in my head (I don't go to that salon any more). My memories are precise images: it's evening, I'm sitting in the salon chair, the bleached-blonde kid who's really good is drying my hair, or the big, burly guy with no patience finishes in two minutes, all the while the smell of Chinese food is wafting in because everyone around here never stops working and the salons in Chinatown are always open, even on Sunday, even until 9 p.m.

Giulia replied, 'You can't calculate everything now. You'll figure it out when it happens, you'll see. Don't worry.' But I couldn't not worry. I barely know what maths is and I was making all these calculations. Pointless calculations, thinking back now, knowing that it took me years to get pregnant. Pointless calculation after calculation after calculation because, no matter what calculation I'd come up with, when things happened they happened all at once. A fireball of words and babies blasted 100,000,000 kilometres per hour from the furthest planet in the universe all the way into me. A spectacular fireball that would create and destroy everything. A terrible and beautiful ball of fire.

(But then, as my publication date looms, while my betas are sky high, while I spend my days at home alone – Andrea is on set, on set, on set – the thought that I'm betraying my publisher by being pregnant starts to take over. The thought that they've been working with me on this novel for years, they trust me, yet I haven't told them I'm pregnant. The thought that being pregnant means betraying the people who trust in me, in the rigour of my work. Because from this point on there is no separation between my feelings about the pregnancy and about the novel. About what's happening with the novel and what's happening with the pregnancy. I have nightmares about the pregnancy. I have nightmares where my editor says to me, 'you betrayed us.' I don't talk to Andrea about the nightmares. I talk to Giulia. I talk to Bianca, another friend I eventually tell. Bianca's the kind of friend who can convince me of anything. She tries to reassure me, saying, 'If it'd been twins, OK, that might be reason to worry. But it's one. And you can take a newborn anywhere, you can take them along on your entire tour, no problem.' 'Without a nanny?' I reply. 'Or family to help me, a babysitter?' I don't have the money to be the ambitious woman I am and a mother too. I've always known that. Bianca tries to reassure me, saying, 'You'll see. When the time comes, you'll figure out a way.' Exactly what way would that be? I have nightmare after nightmare, I'm split in two, two people fighting one against the other. I think that I want this child more than anything. Then I think that the baby is due in August and that I'll have to do all the book promotion while I'm pregnant. That I'll never work again the way I do now.)

Writing this book isn't good for me.

It dredges up everything I've tried to put out of my mind these past months, into the part of me dammed off from the world.

Today, 4 November 2021, for the first time in almost a year, I made a serious mistake. I took an ovulation test, which measures the LH levels in your urine so you can figure your peak ovulation dates to plan intercourse for when you're most likely to conceive. There's an internet myth that if your period is late, a positive ovulation test means that you're pregnant. I'm late, only by one day, and I'm not even regular, but I don't have any pregnancy tests at home, only ovulation ones. So I take it. It comes out positive. I'm convinced I'm pregnant. That I succeeded naturally (after years of failure), thanks to the form of magical thinking that says once you've given up all hope of getting pregnant the natural way, you get pregnant the natural way.

The ovulation test comes out positive so I find an excuse to go out and rush to the pharmacy – one in another neighbourhood, where they don't know me – and buy a Clearblue test. The high-tech kind that can detect pregnancy even six days before a missed period. The kind that promises 99 per cent accuracy and shows your result on a digital display. I run into a coffee bar and do it in the bathroom. I mess up. The test is invalid. The error message is a little open book (it's true). I go to a work lunch. I'm completely zoned out, convinced I'm pregnant. The work lunch ends and I go home. I buy another test on the way. I lock myself in the bathroom. I don't have the nerve to show Andrea this stupid side of me. The result takes forever to come up. NOT PREGNANT appears in huge letters after what feels like an hour. I hadn't done this to myself until I started writing this book. This book isn't good for me.

I don't know how to explain it. The only image I can think of is a racehorse waiting at the starting gate, pawing the ground, anxious to go. For these months since everything has happened, I'm standing there behind the starting gate. Not a day, not an hour goes by that I don't think about it. A child.

I'm standing there at the gate, waiting for my time.

Now, since I started writing this book, the starting gates have opened and I'm off. I can feel the wind in my mane and the ground under my hooves, and even though I don't know what I'm running towards, I'm running like a madwoman, like a demon, I'm racing, again, same as a year ago, same as two years ago. The only thing in my mind is the finish line and nothing will stop me. Which is why, today, I took another pregnancy test. For no reason. I hadn't, since last December – nearly a year. Today I took three, to be exact. Obsessive-compulsively. As if repetition would change the outcome.

It's been a day since I wrote about taking those tests. I got my period. This book has an effect on me.

This whole story is a story about blood. I didn't have a period from April 2021 until 8 October 2021. I start writing this book on 7 October. On 8 October, after seven months, my period returned.

It's true. I'm not making any of this up. I have to be honest. This book, for better, for worse, is affecting me.

On 23 December, I go back to Dr S. I'm at 6 weeks and 2 days. I've learned a lot so far, including how to calculate gestational age (not an easy calculation, especially for me). That pregnancy isn't like real life where you can say 'a couple of weeks,' or 'two months.' Everything has to be said with exactitude. You have to be precise not only with the weeks (six weeks, never a month and a half, for example), but also with the days. I am at 6 weeks and 2 days. Today, in addition to the yolk sac, the embryo should be visible. If the embryo is there. If it's not an ectopic pregnancy. If it's not dead, since the highest probability of it happening is within the first three months (I try to convince myself of the worst, clearly, but deep down I'm sure everything is going to be amazing).

Meanwhile, shortly after the transfer, when we were still in the two-week wait and didn't know whether I was pregnant or not, Andrea and I bought a Christmas tree for the first time. I had never had one, neither before him nor with him. I had never decorated for Christmas. I don't know if he ever did, before me. It just never occurred to us, the whole six years we'd been living together. The tree we got was small, scraggly, with just a few decorations – baubles that, one by one, almost all break because the tree is so short we constantly trip over it, and laugh – with an ugly, lopsided ballerina on top (which I chose, I always wanted to be a dancer). It wasn't a conscious decision.

We didn't think *Oh, great, the transfer worked, hopefully we're pregnant, we'd better put up a Christmas tree.* One Saturday afternoon in December, Andrea and I were driving home and he said to me, 'How about we get a Christmas tree?' Or maybe I said it to him. I notice that across from Santa Maria Maggiore there's an entire store filled with awful Christmas decorations. We wander down the aisles, sharing the tackiest trinkets we find. Those are the ones we buy. I insist on topping our tiny tree with this floppy, ugly ballerina. Once we're home, once we've decorated it, we'll take pictures of that little Christmas tree and send them to our friends, who will laugh. I'll insist on playing the dumbest, corniest Christmas songs while we decorate. If you're going to do something, you might as well do it all the way. At one point Andrea says, 'OK, we've got into the Christmas spirit, now turn off the music, I'm begging you.' And I dance around him singing 'Last Christmas' and he says, 'you're such a dope,' and laughs.

It's really Christmas. Maybe for the first time in my life, it's nice. Maybe it's lockdown, not being able to travel outside the region or even outside the city; maybe it's that I have no outlet for my all-consuming hunger for adventure and risk (usually during Christmas I drag Andrea on trips to warm destinations halfway across the world, wonderful to me, wearying for him); maybe it's that even if I wanted to I couldn't hop on a plane to Mexico, or go to Bari to see my family, or organise anything here. Maybe it's that I'm happy and hopeful about this thing – I don't want to call it anything more specific – that might happen. But this year for the first and only time in my life I make peace with all the holiday rituals, even if not consciously.

I'm here, fully here, and nowhere else, when I'm the one who is always elsewhere. Who is always restless. Who, like a five-year-old girl, as Andrea always tells me (though I disagree), always wants another adventure, and another, and another. Maybe it's that this is my adventure.

It's 23 December and Christmas is everywhere. We're still working on the book launch. Now, a year later, I look back at those texts, those emails, me writing 'It's going to be our year' (which I think about the book, and I think about all the rest but can't say, have decided not to say); I look back at them because I have to, because I've decided to write this book. If I hadn't, I would never have looked at them again. But you can't spare yourself if you want to write a book. You want to be able to write without pity for anyone, not even yourself.

It's 23 December and Christmas is everywhere, my work emails and texts from those days are excited, ecstatic, full of ideas. I'm divided between the novel and this thing that's happening to me although I'm not really divided. Maybe, for the first time, I'm a mix. I answer my emails and texts and then I go to see Dr S.

Prati is decked out in sparkling light installations. Andrea is driving through the streets of Rome to Dr S.'s office, and I wish I knew what he's thinking, what he's feeling. Any time I ask him he mutters something that frightens me. If I didn't know otherwise, I'd never guess that he was going to the most important doctor's appointment of his life – or at least, a doctor's appointment that could change his life completely. I say nothing, and part of me is terrified that something

I've always thought – Andrea will be a much better father than I'll be a mother – is true (I'll be a disaster of a mother, and he doesn't want to be a father, I forced him). But another part of me doesn't care about that. Doesn't care about anything except what's happening at this moment. Now, a year later, writing about it makes my heart race. I'm there again.

Today it's 24 November 2021. A year ago I was in Y for the transfer. I haven't written since 6 November. I just couldn't. I sought out frustrating, low-paying jobs so I could tell myself, I don't have time to get my head into this book. Now I have no excuses. I have less work, I'm home alone all day. This morning I told myself, it's time to start writing again. I hadn't even realised that today it's been a year since everything started. It's 4 p.m. From 11 a.m. to now, I've done nothing. I didn't work on other stuff, I didn't make any phone calls, I didn't eat, I didn't read, I didn't take a walk, I didn't see a friend. I didn't do anything. I tried to summon the courage to start writing again. I smoked the whole time.

This book is an immersion. Into the bleakest darkness I've ever felt, but also into a period so wonderful, so unbelievably wonderful given everything I had hanging over my head, so stupidly wonderful given everything I knew could happen, that it hurts more to write about the good than the bad. But it's an immersion in a time of hope, too. To remember that it existed. Yet I don't know if I want to remember that it existed.

I'm forcing myself to write. If I ever manage to finish this book, I'll come back here, to this page, and say: you had the courage all along.

It always takes courage to write a book. Lots of things take courage. To write a book, you have to have faith. How can a person who has lost faith keep writing?

There are no patients at Dr S.'s office, only Cinzia, his receptionist who I've become friends with, and Dr S., who flashes us a big smile and says, 'Come in.' Outside it's dark. A Christmas evening darkness; finally, it's Christmastime to me too. The light displays twinkle everywhere.

'Relax, Antonella,' Dr S. tells me. His voice is very soothing. He always seems to understand me better than Andrea.

Andrea sits down by the desk. I undress and go to the ultrasound area. Dr S. calls Andrea over:

'Come. You should look too.'

Andrea, typing something on his phone, seems to get up reluctantly, seems reluctantly to come and sit down next to me, on my right. I'm on the table, legs open. Dr S is on the other side, my left, at the ultrasound machine. 'You should be able to see now. Perhaps hear the heartbeat as well. But we'll just listen for a second,' Dr S. says. 'It's a bit soon.'

We're there at Christmastime, in the evening, at aperitivo hour, with the dark outside and this soft light inside.

Dr S. inserts the wand. I look at the monitor. Dr S. repeats to Andrea, 'You should look too.'

We all look at the monitor. Something's there, although I can't tell what, and neither can Andrea. Dr S.'s face changes. 'There are two,' he says.

What?

All our joy comes to a halt at that screen. Twins ... at the clinic they'd told me all kinds of things against a multiple pregnancy. Twins ... I'm not ready, I can't have twins, I have to work, how will I manage with work? How will I manage with life? Giulia and Bianca told me that with one it's still possible to work, you can still promote a book, but with two? They say with two it'd be impossible. I'm selfish. I'm a degenerate mother. I'm not happy, not even for a second (later I will read everywhere about women who are elated, who are over the moon about their twin pregnancies – not me; later I will read everywhere about mothers saying, 'I wasn't expecting it, but I'm thrilled'). I'm a degenerate mother, perhaps not even a mother at all. I've inherited the non-motherhood gene. I don't feel happy even for an instant.

Something happens to my right, where Andrea is sitting, but I don't see because I'm looking the other way at the monitor. I hear Dr S. say, 'Are you all right, son?'

I turn to Andrea and I don't remember, now I don't remember what he looked like. The look on his face. All I remember is Dr S.'s question and Andrea saying, 'Did you say two?'

We had said it was only one gestational sac, that there was only one embryo. Only later will I hear Dr S.'s concerns. For now he says, 'Let's listen to the heartbeat for a second.'

Just a second.

First one beat. Then the other. There's a heart line like the wiretaps on the crime shows I watch all the time.

Just a second. First one heart. Then the other. There are two.

That heartbeat. Those heartbeats.

I've heard a heartbeat twice before, during the ultrasounds of the babies I didn't want, that I aborted. In those situations, it was the gynaecologist's last-ditch effort to convince me to reconsider. It wasn't right for him to do that, I know. But it was quick, and I just wanted to get it over with. This time, those heartbeats. Today, as I write, to think about those heartbeats makes me want to abandon this book and never write anything again. The heartbeat. Like a message from E.T.

We leave the ultrasound area in shock. It's not fair, I think, this was supposed to be a joyous moment, the first time hearing the heartbeat of a baby that I can keep (be honest, OK: that I want to keep), and instead it wasn't. I don't want twins. My life will be over, with twins. The sky before was a tender blue-black; now it's just dark.

We leave Dr S.'s room in shock. I look at Andrea but can't tell what he's thinking. Dr S. says to Cinzia, 'It's twins!' She looks at me, not sure what to say. Andrea goes to the bathroom. 'He's probably escaping out the window,' Dr S. says, laughing for the first time. I laugh too, but I'm despondent.

Dr S. doesn't know, nor do I know, what will happen a few minutes later.

'See you in a week, Antonella,' he says. 'Come on, it'll be fine with two.' Then he turns serious and says: 'They may not both make it to the third month. There is little chance that they'll both survive.'

He thinks he's giving me bad news but because I'm a shitty mother I think: I hope only one survives. Because I'm the shittiest mother there is.

*

We walk out of there with our scans and it feels like a different world from the one we left walking in. It's off. It's wrong. Quietly, we get into the car. I'm thinking all the worst possible things. 'What do we do now?' I say to Andrea. I assume he's even more upset than me. He turns to me and says, 'It's amazing that it's two. We can do this. We'll move to a bigger place. We'll use all our money to help us get by. It'll be great, you'll see. They'll be our Gianni and Pinotto' (these are the Italian names of Abbott and Costello). 'Let's just hope that they look like me.' He laughs.

Suddenly the sky brightens and we float home on cloud nine. If Andrea says we can do it, we can do it, it will be great, he's right. We float home; I was about to die and instead he showed me a way, he gave me courage, he brought me joy. The complete opposite of what I had expected.

I go clothes shopping for Christmas because I'm happy (and trying them on I think, 'Hey, world! You have no idea that I. AM. A. MOTHER!'). When I get home I call Giulia and exclaim, 'I'm having twins!' She laughs a bit hysterically, afraid I'm about to burst into tears, but I'm happy, Andrea said we can do this and so we'll find a way. Giulia starts talking about how two are better than one, they can grow up together, support each other. She lists everyone she knows who has twins. It shouldn't be done, it's too soon, but Giulia's partner Roberto writes to Andrea: 'Holy shit, great news, my friend!' with a string of emojis, and Andrea laughs, and I laugh, we go crazy. We'll go crazy many times throughout this story.

A Christmas package arrives from my mother. It's a couple of sweaters and a necklace: I really like them (I still wear them now, a year later). I call my mother to thank her and tell her, 'These are such nice gifts!'

She's happy, she has no idea what is going on with me, but I'm happy and she's happy and while we usually have trouble really telling each other things, this time we communicate not with words but through joy. Mamma, I think, I can't wait to tell you that you're going to become a grandmother.

It's the sweetest night I remember. It's the night when Andrea becomes a father. For the first time, there are four of us.

Now, a year later, I'm writing this book.

I ask Andrea: what's your favourite moment that you remember from our pregnancy? (I don't actually say 'pregnancy', of course, we don't use these kinds of words; even now when we talk about it I say 'that story', 'that thing', 'those months'; I never say pregnancy, mother, father, baby, pregnant, nothing like that; I can't; but for a book you need the right words and, for the first time, I must have the courage to use them.) He mumbles in reply, 'When we found out it was twins.'

The worst moment (what seemed then like the worst moment) was actually the best. We were intoxicated with these twins. Though not because of me. Without Andrea's encouragement, I would have gone on despairing, thinking of having two. It was his courage. It was because of him that I became a mother.

A few days later I go to have photos taken for the new book. A very talented friend of ours takes me to a hotel in the centre of Rome for the shoot. All the pictures that appear online and in the press for my new book were taken with what I thought were my two babies in my belly. I worry: Am I bloated? Will I look bad? I've been throwing up constantly. My photographer friend makes it fun, helps me feel at ease. It's a wonderful morning, with this book about to come out and this secret inside. I remember taking the photos for my last book. It was an awful time for me. Not because of the book, and nothing to do with children, just me. And you can see it in the pictures. But this time I'm elated.

As I get my photo taken, as I do the first interviews, as the publisher sends me the draft of the marketing campaign, as reactions start coming in from the journalists, writers, trusted friends we sent advance copies to, as we're constantly in contact, while all this is going on, I'm pregnant. I feel strong, pumped for the release, I can't contain myself. Giulia was right: everything's going to be fine, the book and the pregnancy. There are two hearts beating inside me, besides a third, my own. Those photos hold all the emotion of those days, those months. To look at them closely is to understand everything (now, those photos come to life as ghosts with mocking smiles: here is what you once were and are no more).

*

After that 23 December, we call them Gianni and Pinotto. Not sweet names, nicknames, terms of endearment. Gianni and Pinotto, a couple of comedians, as Andrea named them when he met them. We don't know that we won't be calling them by those names for long.

You have a ton of secrets, and I have none, goes a song I like.

Once a boyfriend told me, 'Those lyrics always make me think of you.'

If Andrea were like that old boyfriend, maybe he would tell me the same. But he's not one for such long phrases.

On 23 December, I write in my chat with Ada and Bianca: 'It's twins!' They send congratulations and say it's going to be wonderful. 'Two and through! You'll be set for life!' We laugh and laugh and I'm on top of the world.

For Christmas, we go to Giulia's. We sing, we dance, I feel afraid again that I won't be able to be a mother. I eat oysters. I drink wine. Andrea cuts himself shucking an oyster. Panic for a moment, then calm. I try to calm down too. Maybe I do, by the time we go to bed. I sleep on the couch (I feel safer sleeping alone), my hand on my belly with the two of them. The future is unthinkable. I don't know how to begin to picture it. That night, and always, it's like a marvellous fairy tale in flashes, or more than a fairy tale; other times, it's too blurry to make out. Others still, it's too scary. I wonder if Gianni and Pinotto are sleeping, floating, or what.

That Christmas, despite being stuck at home because of Covid, despite not being able to leave the city, despite the dangers of a multiple pregnancy (which we truly don't think about, because it still seems incredible), was the best Christmas of my life. We rewatch *Harry Potter* and all the Christmas movies, we have dinner and lunch with Emilio and Carlo (the ones I went to Sperlonga with in August), who live so close by that we can each sneak over to the others' flat. They don't know what's going on, but I do, and with them, these twins are safe. Everyone is a part of these two children growing inside me every day: everyone who loves me is in there; even if they don't know I'm pregnant, they're there. I learn for the first time in my life that you don't need people to know about a situation to be a support, a comfort, a help. And to make you happy.

On 28 December I go for my first ultrasound with the doctor I've been seeing at the Y clinic, at her Rome office. I haven't told her that I've already done two ultrasounds with Dr S.

When I get there, she welcomes me with a big smile. Then it fades. 'What about the father?' she asks. 'Where is he?' *The father.* None of your fucking business. That *Where is he?* oozes judgment. Of the absentee father she's never seen with me. *What about the father? Where is he?* Subtext: so the father isn't here, again. How many times, in those months, would she or the other doctors mangle sentences for this phantom father. It worked: they managed to plant the seed of resentment in me as well. Another woman I never wanted to become: the mother who feels abandoned by her husband who's always working or who doesn't consider their child (or doesn't want it). How many times would Giulia, Ada or Bianca say to me, did you tell her off? Her, or any of the other tactless people I would encounter. As I've said, I don't want to tell anyone off.

The doctor says she's prepping the video to record the heartbeat *for the dad.* She says, 'And now we'll finally find out if it's one or two.' And I see her smirking with schadenfreude because she thinks I'm worried. But I'm not worried. I'm ready. I already know it's twins. I don't let on. I can't wait to see them again. Gianni and Pinotto. I can't wait to hear their hearts again.

I undress. I keep my phone with me, ready to record them and their hearts. I lie back on the table. I open my legs. She inserts the wand and I'm holding the phone and she is stunned. I'm ready to take a video and I know why she's stunned: it's twins. You don't scare me, bitch, I already know that a twin pregnancy is much more difficult, but I'm happy, I'm ready, I'm prepared for all the stressful things you're going to tell me, I can handle it.

'I don't understand how this is possible,' she says, 'but there are three.'

'But I only transferred two embryos,' I say in disbelief. 'How can there be three?' I'm sure she's going to reply, Oh, sorry, I was mistaken. I know it.

'There are three,' she repeats.

I would never record that ultrasound or those heartbeats.

We're out of our minds, as I've said, and nonetheless I have a clear memory of that day. The day the shit hit the fan.

The doctor tells me that, somehow, both embryos attached, and one of them split? (*split*? What is this, a sci-fi movie?) – somehow, I have a triple pregnancy, and one of this sort is almost impossible to carry to term. Triplets, I can't even contemplate. The doctor illustrates all the horrors associated with triple pregnancies, the very high probability that one of them won't make it, or two, or all three, or all four, including me. It's too dangerous, she tells me. The likelihood of even one surviving is low, and that I myself won't survive is also a possibility.

While everything around me is spinning and my ears are ringing and I just keep thinking, you have to listen to what she's saying, you have to listen carefully because you're going to have to report all this to Androo, she calls in another gynaecologist to advise. They yell at me for implanting two embryos, really lay into me (and this other doctor is the guy who told me, 'you have to gamble if you want to win'; 'Did you tell him off?' my friends will ask; 'No,' again); the doctors tell me that if I believe in God I can try to keep the three babies ('They said *what* to you?! Did you tell them off?' 'No'), but that otherwise I'll have to think about getting a *reduction*.

*

Reduction means that – well, I don't know how to write it, I don't even know how to say it in my head – reduction means that one of the three foetuses will be ... killed? eliminated? How can I say it? What words am I supposed to use? What words can I use? What are the words I want to use in this book, in my writing? I learn, increasingly, that the medical field is full of euphemisms (here I thought medical language was precise, the type of language I prefer above all else, language that doesn't sugar-coat anything, not even in a novel; language that doesn't sugar-coat anything, though in my own life I lie and sugar-coat everything). I'll have to have a *reduction*, then. Unless I leave it up to God, I have no choice. Unfortunately, I don't have God. My mother does. But my mother doesn't know about any of this. She will never know. If I don't leave it up to God, medicine says a reduction is my only option. And even then, the likelihood of this pregnancy coming to term is still very low. They tell me that to do the *reduction* I'll have to go to Milan. They yell at me, 'This a problem for us too, the directors of the Y clinic aren't going to be happy, how are we going to explain it to them?' ('What?! Did you tell them off then?' 'No'), and then they tell me they want nothing more to do with this pregnancy, that they can refer me to a specialist for multiples but that's it, they can't do anything else for me. I listen and listen and try to remember everything I'll have to report to Andrea and Dr S., and I clutch the scans of my triplets and I listen and I tell myself, stay here, don't pass out, don't lose your head, pay attention to everything they say. I listen as they paint this whole horrific picture and as they yell at me I say nothing and when they finish I ask, 'But are they all right?' 'Yes, they're all right, all three of them.'

When they send me away I must look so pale they're afraid I'm going to pass out. But they don't have me sit down, they don't take me anywhere, they just ask, 'How did you get here? Scooter? Car? You're very pale and shouldn't drive.' Obviously since I'm pregnant I don't ride scooters any more. I took a taxi there.

No need for any help, I say, I'm leaving. In the taxi I get a message from Andrea who's all happy. 'So how'd it go? How did she react?' I write back, 'You don't understand. It's triplets.'

But I don't really believe that it's a tragedy, despite everything the gynaecologist told me: haemorrhaging, deaths in utero, my own death – I don't really believe it's a tragedy, I never will, and neither throughout this entire story will Andrea. We will do everything for these three. We will do everything they tell us to. But deep down, neither of us really believes that it can go wrong. Maybe because no one ever really believes they're in the eye of the storm. Maybe it's because we're the parents, and we can't believe it. And I'm the mother.

I get home and Andrea is a wreck. I write Dr S. a very long message, tell him about Milan, the multiples clinic, and the reduction, and that I'm scared, and I ask him what to do. Then, exactly one minute later, I write him another message: 'They're fine. All three of them.' Up until two months ago, I didn't have anyone inside me. Now there are three. All I want is for them to be OK. As I'm scrolling on my phone an hour and a half later, Dr S. calls. But I can't answer because in the meantime fate intervenes again.

While Andrea and I are at home – lockdown, Covid, Christmas vacation, the first online promos from my publisher, the likes, my excitement about the book, then my desperation, then my happiness about those babies, whoever they are, however many there are – we're looking at each other and I'm trying to explain everything they told me at the clinic (my impression is we have the same response: our minds can't really contemplate what's happening) and I get a call from a very dear friend of mine (as I'm writing this, I'm realising how many very dear friends I have and love).

His name is Marco. He spent Christmas with his parents. He came back home and felt weird. Then he got a fever. He took a test. It was positive.

What are the odds in life of so many extraordinary events happening at once and all being interconnected? Point-zero-something, but this entire story is about point-zero-something chances of things where you tell yourself the likelihood is so slim there's no way it'll happen and then the point-zero-something trumps the ninety-nine-point-something and wins every time.

When Marco calls me, I'm still holding the ultrasound of the triplets. I'm trying to explain everything to Andrea. I answer the phone, and Marco says, 'I have Covid' and everything goes dark. This is the period when Covid is extremely dangerous, when you risk going into intensive care, and Marco, who has just visited his elderly parents, keeps saying, 'I've killed them', and I imagine him home alone – he lives by himself – torturing himself with worry and guilt, on top of being ill.

And there's a kicker.

Because I'm a degenerate mother, I had a drink with Marco two days ago. We were at his house (inside), with the windows closed. Because I'm always cold, he lit the fireplace for me. We ate from the same bag of crisps. So fine. I'm crazy. But what's done is done. (I want to delete what I wrote – the truth – and replace it with a generic 'I saw Marco,' without detailing how reckless I had been. But I promised to be honest.) I end the call and tell Andrea, 'Marco has Covid.' I can't have Covid. I can't, because I'm pregnant. I can't even quarantine; I have to see the multiples specialist. I have to figure out what to do ('as soon as possible, or sooner, sooner than possible!' the gynaecologist at the centre had yelled at me) with everything that's going on with me. I can't have Covid. I'm pregnant.

It's night, in Rome. We're in a taxi. We found a private lab where they do tests after hours. It's now that Dr S calls me, but I can't answer because I'm on my way to take the test. Andrea and me, in the cab, hand in hand. How can I explain that now this memory is sweet? Of course, we're terrified of everything that's happening. But because it's all too much, we're brave. I once read that courage comes to you when you can't think any more. A true hero doesn't think, but acts. Maybe at this point we are immersed. We will be very brave through a certain part of this story. I remember two of us in that speeding taxi, hand in hand, not only

Rome flashing by but all our fears too – triple pregnancy, Covid – and it all slides into the background and our only thought is: they are there, their pulse is strong, they're inside me. They'll be born. We don't need to say it out loud. I'm still holding the ultrasound pictures. I hand them to Andrea, in the cab, indicating each: one, two, three. He squeezes my hand, pulls me close, says, 'Hello, Aldo, Giovanni and Giacomo.' (If you know, you know.)

We take four tests. One rapid each. One PCR each. It costs a fortune. We can't be positive. It's impossible. When we leave the clinic, it's 9.30 p.m.

We slide into the taxi. We don't stop squeezing each other's hand. Then, for the first time, Andrea pulls his hand away and places it on my belly. I put mine there too, on top of his. On top of the four of them.

I call Dr S. back. He answers right away even though it's late. That fatherly voice, firm and reassuring – if only he knew what that voice meant to me. He tells me that the situation is very complicated, and that the reduction is necessary. But he's not alarmed or angry at me for transferring two embryos. His voice is calm. He tells me we won't go to Milan, but to London. London is the best place for this type of procedure, he says. The success rates are very high. I have to remain calm. (I don't know how often, throughout this whole thing, Dr S. kept his concerns to himself so as not to worry me; I've only got the occasional glimpse, like the little pieces of evidence a burglar accidentally leaves behind; but I know that he always told me what I needed to know and kept the horrors to himself, that on this call now there's no sign of anything else, just his reassurance.) He says we're going to make it.

I tell Andrea, 'We're going to make it!' And we hug. We don't want to think about how 'making it' without intervention means that one or two of these embryos won't survive past the first trimester (which is very likely, as the Y gynaecologist, Dr S., and every doctor will tell me; usually in these multiple pregnancies one or more don't survive); while 'making it' with medical help means *reducing* one of our children. We don't think about it because magical thinking (though it's not magical this time, this time it's the human will to survive, or no, it's not the human will to survive: it's denial) tells us we're going to be all right.

There, that's the word: denial. We will get through these months on dogged, rigid denial.

Between fear of Covid and this new reality buzzing in our heads, we spend the night in a state of incredulity. 'That's not possible' is the phrase I'll say most throughout this story.

Andrea says, 'You have to eat.' He's referring to all four of us. The gynaecologist at the Y clinic told me, 'I don't know how you can stay standing with triplets in there. You should be in bed vomiting your guts out.' But I feel good, stronger than ever. The five of us eat, at midnight, in the warmth of a house that, despite everything, is wonderful (and I've always hated the loaded concept 'home'). Our crooked little tree sparkles.

*

We get our rapid test results. Negative. Overnight we get the PCR. Negative. The next morning, Marco's PCR: negative. His rapid was a false positive.

Marco has no idea how happy I am. For us, but also for him. Thinking of him in that house, freaking out alone. A terrible thought. But we are fine, all five of us. And he's OK, too.

See, God, see, world, see, whoever you are, that we're going to make it?

Since everything happened, I never put my hand on my belly. Ever.

If Andrea's hand lands there, I move it.

This year, we left our ragtag little tree with its ridiculous decorations in the box. We didn't even say we weren't going to put it up. We both know that it wasn't an oversight: every street and every building was covered in Christmas lights. It was simply that when the time came, neither of us mentioned it.

Then after a while Andrea said to me: 'What about the tree? Should we put it up?'

And I felt bad because I thought we'd been thinking the same thing without saying it. But what do I expect, that there's a crystal ball and he'll understand even if I don't say anything?

So I said, 'I don't want to. It reminds me of last year.'

That annoyed him. 'You can't always think of last year. We can't not do anything ever again because everything reminds you of last year.'

I said, 'OK, let's put it up.'

We didn't.

What happens is:

Dr S. tells me he's going to call London, and not to worry. He'll take care of everything.

On the 30th, I go for another ultrasound. The situation revealed in this ultrasound surpasses my imagination, and not only mine, but also Andrea's, Dr S.'s and the gynaecologist's from Y. It's not that one embryo implanted and the other one split, but that only one embryo implanted and then split into three. It's called monochorionic triamniotic pregnancy. There is only one yolk sac, as Dr S. saw at the first ultrasound. There is only one placenta and three embryos. I will only understand later what that really means. Dr S. says not to worry and that he'll take care of everything. He repeats that the chance of all three surviving is minimal (we don't know what to hope for). The Y centre, Dr S. and the other doctors all say the same thing: they've never seen this before. There's no real literature on it either. It's too rare. You were unlucky, Antonella – how many times would I hear that phrase in the coming months. The doctors, the gynaecologists, the surgeons, the ultrasound technicians we see constantly will be dumbstruck: never seen this before. A single embryo triplicating. We know, we hear it's a tragedy. But we don't understand it. It's impossible. It can't be. These are the phrases we repeat the most, that are repeated most often by people who know. So what do we do now?

We go to appointments and despair. But as soon

as we leave it's like we forget everything. We only remember this feeling of euphoria. I don't know how to explain it. Your brain tells you one thing, but there are these three hearts beating (and they're thriving, everyone tells me, all three). But I have to be honest: we hope that one of the three doesn't make it. We are forced to hope for an atrocity.

When I explain to the Y clinic doctor what's going on, she doesn't apologise for telling me that this inconceivable pregnancy is all my fault for having decided to transfer two embryos. (Did you tell that bitch off? No.) Who gives a damn about apologies. We have to worry about surviving.

Once again we ignore Covid restrictions and go to Marco's for New Year's Eve. It's him, his girlfriend, and the five of us. Dr S. told me not to eat any kind of pork, not even sausage. Dinner is sausage. Andrea secretly slides my meat onto his plate. We exchange a smile: our little secret. We stay up playing Risk until dawn. We stick close to the buildings as we walk home, all five of us, trying to keep a low profile in case the police are out. The sunrise is gorgeous, the most beautiful dawn that's ever been.

In early January, Emilio and Carlo get married without telling anyone. There's Covid, and guests aren't allowed. But they invite us for lunch right after the ceremony and tell us there. I'm moved, they're happy. I can't wait to reveal my surprise, the unbelievable news: I'm pregnant. I wonder how they'll react. I constantly imagine telling my friends and how they'll react, and I can't wait. I can't wait to be flooded with love. At one point during that lunch, as I'm sipping what Emilio has taken to calling 'my' Schweppes, I nearly tell them. But I have this dam holding everything in and I can't. But I'd as good as told you, my friends. That day, together, we celebrated everything: your wedding and our children.

My winter coat is worn out. I've had it for fifteen years. So my friend Luca and I go out shopping. I try on a small and it's a bit snug. I hope he'll give me a look and say, 'wait, are you pregnant?' But he wouldn't even suspect it, he knows I tell him everything. I send Giulia a picture: 'What do you think?' She replies, 'Uh ... I don't think this is exactly the time to buy a coat you won't be able to fit into in a month' with a line of hearts and smiling emojis. (I went back to Rinascente this year and bought the coat: another gratuitous show of strength like I've been making since everything happened, like when you burn your skin on purpose to build your tolerance to pain.)

I go in for scans constantly, almost every other day. Dr S. is always present. It could be New Year's, Saturday, Sunday, his day off. He monitors me the whole time, waiting to hear from London. He does let one clue slip: he no longer has me listen to the heartbeat. One time when he steps out of the room I ask another doctor if I can hear it, and those rhythmic pulses make me euphoric, but when Dr S. comes back he becomes stern and asks her, 'Why did you have her listen to the heartbeat?' His colleague points in my direction and says, 'She asked to.' He says nothing. A voice inside me asks: *Why doesn't he want you to hear the heartbeat? Because he's in a hurry. Just because he's in a hurry.*

The embryos, the babies, whatever I'm supposed to call them – they are thriving. They're growing, they're of equal size, their heartbeats are strong, they are securely implanted. The hope that one of them is *resorbed* – what a horrendous term – on its own is minimal. Can it be a *hope* that a child dies? What am I to think? What am I to hope? Really, for at least one to die? How can anyone hope for such a thing? How can anyone not? How can anyone any of it?

I receive the first copies of the book, which is coming out in a matter of days. I give one to Dr S.

The Alpha variant is spreading across Europe. Dr S. tells us that we can't go to London for the reduction. (How is this possible? How is it possible that all this is interconnected? How is it possible that London just so happens to be the place for this procedure and a new variant has arisen in England?) Despairing, I ask: 'What will we do?' He says: 'We'll have to do it in Italy. We'll go to Milan. It will be all right. Maybe it's better this way.'

When he's not home, Andrea sends me texts like, 'What are Aldo, Giovanni and Giacomo up to?' And I'll reply, 'Aldo's sleeping, Giovanni's chilling, Giacomo's stressing.' We've invented personalities for our babies: the idler, the carefree *bon vivant*, the worrier – like me. Giacomo is always worrying, and we make fun of him all the time. 'Invent' isn't the right word – these personalities are real to us. These children exist. And they have their individual traits and quirks.

On 8 January, I go to Milan, to my publisher's office, for the book. I'm excited. The feeling I have about the book and my feeling about this pregnancy are never separate. Doing events usually terrifies me: I stuttered when I was little (and not occasionally, all the time) and though I've improved, sometimes when I'm nervous I stutter or lose my words altogether. So, usually, I'm terrified of events. Of getting stuck mid-sentence or clamming up completely. This time, with this book, I'm not afraid of anything.

My experience with my last book was horrible. I let myself be overwhelmed with terror – over the release, the reviews, the events. Although everything ultimately went well, I fell into a depression and took medication to try to get through it; I lost ten kilos, I couldn't eat or speak. 'I want to soak up all the happiness from this novel that I couldn't get from the last one,' I write to a friend. But this strength, this faith in the present and future, comes from the joy of this pregnancy, even if I don't realise it yet. It seems absurd, it *is* absurd, but all the bad news about our condition filters right through us. It's like when you drain pasta. The water is all the tragedy inflicted upon us. The pasta is the three babies. Only they remain.

I think it's joy, but it's actually hope that has gone black and goes by that same name: denial.

Dr S tries to find a day when they can take me at the hospital in Milan. It could be any day. And I can't choose which. I have to go to this special centre *as soon as possible*, the situation is critical. But on 8 January I'm going to Milan for the book and it's coming out on the 14th; I can't be in hospital. Everything at the same time. I write to Giulia, 'After all these years, I was hoping for something good, something normal. It feels like a dream' (yes, I write dream, I don't know why). 'Or a nightmare,' she replies. 'Yeah.' 'I'm sure you can do everything online.' 'From the hospital?' I say, with an emoji meant to suggest 'how the hell will I do that?' 'In my opinion you need to tell the publisher what's going on and postpone the readings.' 'No. No, that would be impossible. It's all planned out. If I move

anything it'll just be cancelled. That's how these cam-
paigns work. If I reschedule, the book won't do well.
And telling them now ... I'm not going to do that.'
'Just try not to stress and take things as they come.'
'Yeah.' 'If you think about everything at once you won't
be able to do it.' 'I know.'

The hospital in Milan calls. Dr S. has notified them that I'll be in town on 8–9 January for work. I manage to fit everything in (this is also a story about horrible people, or wonderful ones, like Dr S. and the team at the hospital in Milan). Dr S. never forgets that, besides being a pregnant woman in a terribly difficult situation, I'm a writer. He would never tell me, just put the book aside for now and concentrate on this. And it's rare to encounter a professional who considers you as a whole person and not just as a patient.

In the chaos, Dr S. has found me a light. I tell the publisher that when we're done with the book I have to go to a specialist medical centre because I've been struggling with migraines for years (which is true). This is because they're organising my travel, so the book stuff has to be planned around my appointment at the hospital. I make up lie after lie, going on about these headaches, promising to let them know how I'm doing.

Then 8 January comes around and I, eight weeks pregnant, nauseous, with Aldo, Giovanni and Giacomo, leave for Milan.

I have no clue, no one could, what lies ahead for me in these next hours.

I remember arriving at the hotel. I remember feeling euphoric (please don't see me as vapid or crazy; in all these months that I've been describing I have this fire inside, fire that tells me everything's going to be fine, everything, I can't explain it). The concierge who doesn't know I'm a party of four asks for my ID. I take my suitcase up to my room like it's the first time I've been to a hotel. And it is, in a year. Because finally I'm travelling. Because of my book. And because I'm a mother.

I don't think about the hospital.

I go into the publisher's office. There's a temperature check, masks, distancing. On the tables, piles of my book to sign. Aldo, Giovanni and Giacomo are bursting with joy. Or I am. I take a picture and post it on Instagram. I wrote, 'The day has come!' I'm referring to the book, of course. But it's also a secret message to the stars.

It's a fantastic two days at the publisher's even with all the Covid precautions. I hope not to vomit at a key moment. I manage not to, or during breaks. Aldo, Giovanni and Giacomo cheer me on, or don't care (I like to imagine them as happy children paying no heed to their mother). Andrea texts me and asks about them. 'What's Aldo doing?' 'Sleeping.' 'Giacomo?' 'Giacomo is freaking out about the presentation I have to do.' We laugh about his being neurotic and for the first time, I'm not anxious. He's anxious for me.

The next day, before returning to Rome, I go to the hospital.
    I'm going to write this the only way I can write this.
    The publisher books me a taxi and it takes me to

the clinic. The place looks nice, well maintained, and specialises in complex pregnancies. We're going to make it. I go in. I lie back and spread my legs. Transvaginal ultrasound. The doctors couldn't be nicer. The heartbeat (that heartbeat, what a marvel). I start to see hands, feet, head. Here are the hands. Here are the feet. Here is the head. It's an ultrasound of Huck Finn. Three powerful heartbeats, steady, strong. The babies are doing well.

But the situation is deadly serious. 'Are you prepared for an abortion?' a doctor asks me. 'Well . . .' and I start crying, I won't stop crying, for hours, 'we've been trying for years.' *And these are my children,* I don't say. 'It's tragic,' she says. She gives me a smile. But she is very firm and forthcoming. Because I need to know everything. All the possibilities, all the realities, all the risks. If I want to keep them, I have no choice but to have this reduction (unless I want to tempt fate and risk all three dying, even at the sixth, seventh, eighth, or ninth month, or risk them being born with defects, or dying myself). They lay it all out for me (I make sure to understand every detail; Andrea isn't with me). They draw me pictures (I still have them, they're horrifying). They tell me that the best thing is to choose if I want to abort now, at the end of the second month, or if I want to wait until the end of the first trimester and try the reduction. They explain to me that if this wasn't a monochorionic pregnancy, there would only be a 5–10 per cent chance of losing the other two. But in my case – the kind of case they haven't seen in years – the triplets are in the same sac. They're all connected. She draws an alien with tentacles. It's supposed to be my three babies and me. We're all connected. If one dies, the other two could. And even if the reduction goes well and the pregnancy continues, there are so many potential problems. There is TTTS for example, twin-to-twin transfusion syndrome. One of the two could give all its blood to the other, from a certain point on, randomly. If that happens, there's a procedure they try. If it doesn't work, one will die because it runs out of blood, and the other because its heart bursts. Measurements of the head, hands, feet. Here is the heart. I watch it beating.

I listen very carefully. They say a lot of things. They're very caring and comprehensive, but blunt – there's no point in beating around the bush. They illustrate other potential horrors. If you opt for the reduction, the other two have a 40 per cent chance of survival. *40 per cent?* I thought ...

40 per cent. We'll live with these percentages. The chance that a single embryo could split into three are point-zero-zero-zero-who knows. The chance that two survive. The chance that, even if two survive, some disaster strikes. A flash in my brain says: if the inconceivable already happened, that had only a zero-point-zero-zero-zero-who-knows per cent chance of happening, why shouldn't something that's 40 per cent be possible? That 40 per cent seems like nothing and everything. From within the oblivious, stupid hope in which I'm immersed, it seems, at times, like a lot. Acceptable odds. In all these months, we never truly believe that it could all go wrong. Never.

I have a month to decide. If I want to abort. If I want to try. And whether, if it succeeds, I could go through with a twin pregnancy that could end at any moment.

I wrote it the only way I could. I'm sorry, but I just reread 300 messages from those few days to be as precise as possible. I'm sorry, but that's all I can do. I can't say any more than that. The cream-coloured hospital corridor sways under my feet. I walk out of the clinic and it's getting dark and I cry and cry and cry. I head to the train station and I couldn't care less about masks, sanitiser, contagion. I sit in a bar waiting for the train and I don't put on a mask, I don't sanitise my hands, I touch my eyes, I pick up my mask when it falls on the ground, the one I will wear on the train. I couldn't care about a fucking thing. I call Andrea and cry. I call Giulia and cry. Giulia doesn't know what to say. Nobody does. I get on the train and I cry.

That morning, before finding out the whole situation: 'Aldo, Giovanni and Giacomo are scared.' 'They'll be here soon. Isn't it wonderful to think about?' (Andrea's messages kill me, more than my own.) 'What if they all die?' 'Come on, Toni, you can't always assume the worst, and there are three. Don't be so dramatic.' 'But all the doctors say it could happen.' 'Well, for now we'll have to have faith. I'll see you tonight at the station. You, Aldo, Giovanni and Giacomo.' 'They want to separate us, but all four of us will be together forever.' (I hoped not to write that message in this book.)

Then there's the barrage of messages after that appointment. A mix of fear for them, fear for the thousand things to do for the book in these circumstances. Terror. On the train: 'We can do this, Toni. Luckily, you're strong. You always have been.' I don't reply. He goes on: 'Imagine going through this if you were a wimp.' He's trying to make me laugh, and I laugh, out of our minds as we are. 'You're strong, you've always been strong. These are your kids, for fuck's sake, they're strong like you. They won't

101

give up.' 'You think so?' 'I do.' A few hours later: 'I can't take it. And sitting there for an hour having to hear about all that agony, that future despair. It was unbearable.' 'Let's talk about it when you get home. Please, they didn't say it's all over.' 'I dunno ... Either way it's going to be an ordeal. Endless. Disaster at any moment. For nine months.' 'OK, sure. But even if you have to suffer, it could turn out all right, no?' 'Why is there always suffering?' 'Oh, baby, I don't know. You just have to tough it out.' 'I'm sick of toughing it out, I've been toughing it out for so long.' 'But that's just the way it is. No point in thinking otherwise. We'll tough it out together, my love' (if he were a character in a novel, now calling me 'love,' given who he is and how he usually talks, it'd break my heart). 'But the poor things. I dreamed about them last night. There were two of them.' 'What were they doing' 'Blond.' 'That's not an action.' 'In my belly during the ultrasound we could see she had long hair in ringlets and he had a boy's style but wavy like an English lord.' 'It was a boy and a girl?' 'Yes. Though I know it's impossible. With this type of pregnancy they're all identical. Face, body, exactly the same. Think how wild, three identical children' (we downplay, gloss over, going crazy). 'Let's hope they look like me.' 'No, like me.' 'And then what happens in the dream?' 'She was dressed in pink and he was in blue' (with a shocked emoji like, as if we would dress them in pink and blue). He replied: 'Hahahaha' and then after a pause, 'They're cute.' 'And you could see their face and hands perfectly. And they were doing great.' 'Where's poor little number three?' 'Not there' – pause – 'any more.' 'Fuck it. It's going to be OK.' 'Why can't it be normal? Why can't it just be good?' 'It's going to be OK.' And then I tell him about my phone exploding with messages about the book, about Instagram and Facebook, having to write all these enthusiastic replies, I can't handle it (actually it's not that I have to, I want to; I continue to be this split person, even now, at a moment like this – see, you deserved it). I can't handle it (I can't rationally tell whether all this, which seems bad for me, is actually good for me). And then I tell him that

(wait; breathe)

to get a better look the doctors touched and pressed on my belly and they moved. At this point, they move. At this point, they exist. We wanted them so badly. And we want them to stay with us. He says, 'But there's a 40 per cent chance that two will make it. You have to think that this possibility exists.' 'But even if they get through it, there's still a 15–30 per cent chance the remaining two could end up with TTTS or something else and not make it. And these percentages remain the same for the entire nine months.' 'Everybody told us we'd never have three. Yet here they are. They're tough, Toni. These little guys are tough.'

It's 29 December 2021, when I write these last pages. I told Andrea that I'm still writing. He even agreed to read what I've written. I read it out loud to him. I didn't cry. Now he's coming into the living room. He just woke up. Finally, in Rome – where Covid, like in the rest of the world, is raging again – after a week of rain, it's sunny. I spent my morning looking through my messages and emails so as to be precise, to remember everything. To write what had to be written. Andrea comes into the living room and smiles, saying, 'Is there any coffee for me?' And I break my own rules and burst into tears.

Over everything but especially over a message from him I had just reread. A last message from the train.

'The book has to do well,' I write, 'it has to give us strength through this shitshow' (my exact words, honest as ever). 'Yes. It has to,' plus three fingers-crossed emojis. 'Dr S. says to come in for an ultrasound tomorrow morning at clinic Z and bring all my papers.' 'Perfect. That's where my nephew and nieces were born.' I reply with three hearts. And he says, 'And maybe my children too.'

When I get home, we prepare dinner and talk. I tell him everything, I try not to be too explicit while still being precise. I don't show him the horrifying drawings. I have to be a talking robot, I have to be a medical report (I can't try to sway him: please, don't make me abort the only babies I never wanted to abort). At the end I say, we have two options: abort, or wait a month. You need a month because they have to be as formed as possible to see if any of them has problems, and if they do, that's the one they will *reduce*. Twelve weeks is the limit. We'll be at twelve weeks in a month. At the end of this month, if they're all still alive, we'll have to try the reduction. If it works, the possibility that it won't be an easy pregnancy is still very high.' I don't know how precise I am on that part. I don't know whether he ever really understood the almost certain preterm delivery, the extended hospitalisations before birth, the bedrest required – at home or in hospital – often as early as the fifth or sixth month. The possibility that the babies won't survive remains there throughout, the possibility of needing neonatal intensive care, the possibility that the babies, if they are born, will suffer some kind of defect from being born too soon or not developing properly. For months, I study all of this. I will learn that it's rare for twins (not even triplets) in this type of pregnancy to reach the seventh or eighth month. I join a monochorionic diamniotic pregnancy Facebook group (one for triamniotics, that is, for triplets, doesn't exist). There is strength there, and despair. It's much worse than I thought.

I finish my report. I say, 'What do you want to do? Abort or try?' I see a flicker of doubt. I see it distinctly. I don't know what's going through his mind. I see the doubt flicker, I read it, and I can't stand it. 'We're going to try, right?' I say. And my eyes won't permit another answer. 'Of course we're going to try,' he says. 'And we'll succeed,' he adds.

I feel like Voldemort controlling people's thoughts.

What are you going to do?

Friends ask. I say I can't have an abortion. They agree. (I don't know if they say that because they really think so or just want to be supportive; what can you say to someone who's struggling like this.)

Have you told your mother?

My friends prod me. You need help, they say. You can't keep this to yourself. You need help. But I'm in a world nobody can understand. To open my mouth and speak means making everything real. I can't speak.

At least your sister, then. You need someone close to you.

But I already have people close to me who know, and others who I can't involve. I can't open my mouth. I can't speak.

Causing my parents, my sister pain – I can't do that. Not for them: for me. It hurts too much. I don't want that.

Tell your publisher. Let them help you.

I know that they would help. But I still feel like I'm betraying them. It's not based on anything, this thought, but it's as real as the coffee I can't drink any more, even the smell of it nauseates me, and I love how the smell of it nauseates me so much. I'll never stop, throughout this whole story, clinging to my novel above all else (not above my children, but above everything else, yes; not above my children, but fortunately no one has asked me to choose: your children or your book).

I'm convinced that having to work on the launch and all the events and interviews, now of all times, is going to destroy me. That having these two things mixed up and coinciding is a curse. Once it's too late, I'll understand. Not having the option of giving up, not being able to reveal what's going on to my publisher, is the only thing that will keep me from going insane. It doesn't even matter that it's a book: it could be anything I care about to the same degree. It just has to be something of my own. It will save my sanity.

Up till now, up to this moment in which I'm writing, I thought I was so brave not to put the book aside under those circumstances. I thought so even while it was going on: you're so brave. But I said that to write I have to be honest – here, and only here. And so I have to take myself down a notch. It wasn't bravery. My work gave me life as never before. The beautiful maelstrom of the book gave me life and I transferred it to my three children. The beautiful, absolutely beautiful maelstrom of my children gave me life that I transferred to my book.

It's not bravery. It's not survival.

There's a certain image that always comes to mind. A leech. A leech that sucks and sucks at your blood until you're light-headed. And you give in and close your eyes and what a relief it is when you finally faint.

*

I admonish my friends, don't talk about sad things. We pretend everything is fine. But I'm terrified of breaking down. I don't want to break down. Photo at Week 8 and 5 days, for Ada and Bianca, with my belly out, in profile, as pregnant women do. 'Do you guys think I've gained weight or is it possible that I'm showing a little?' They respond enthusiastically: 'You can tell! Of course you can tell – it's three in there!'

I wear a long skirt to all my readings. The trousers I have don't fit any more. Bianca told me, 'You'll see, you'll just stop wearing them naturally.' Messages filled with hearts and smileys.

(When all this is over, exactly two days before all this is over, my mother who watches all my events online asks: how come you're always in a skirt, you never wear skirts. After that, I try to wear trousers, even if they feel tight. Because I can't have my mother thinking I'm pregnant; I couldn't handle that. I didn't see my parents from when I found out I was pregnant until I was able to fake a smile.)

It's been a few days since I got back from Milan. We've fallen back into delusion. Into stupid black hope. It's not even hope. It's conviction. Everything is going to be all right. We don't even think about how the first step is to reduce them from three to two. We text about them. Jokingly. And about the book. 'It's in the *Corriere!*' the first review of my novel, on 10 January, four days before publication. 'How is it?' 'Great!' 'Where are you?' 'In the living room' – I often sleep by myself in the living room. It's early morning. 'Why are you texting me if we're both in the house?' 'Because I couldn't wait.'

12 January.

'Can you pick up some of those Brioschi antacid tablets? And that lemon-ginger soda that's in the fridge by the entrance?' (everything makes me throw up, soda and lemon help; now, I can't stand the sight of them). 'What else?' 'Yogurt. And those gross rice cake things.' 'OK, which brand?' (he sends me a picture). 'Whichever. Actually, the lemon one.' (We'll buy a thousand jars of Brioschi, there's a half-used one here at home, every time I see it I think about throwing it away but don't want to – it's a combination of: *I don't want to just throw it away, I want to smash it in a million pieces*, and of: *what if I need it again later?* Again with this black hope? And then: *if I throw it away, it really happened; if I don't throw it*

*away maybe it's just randomly there, who knows who
bought it or what for.)*

I have to pack for Milan, 'But I'm sleepy, and
Aldo, Giovanni and Giacomo are pissed off. They
wanted to go on set with you.' 'Come if you feel
up to it, but it's going to be a long day.' 'I can't'
(resentment, incomprehension). And later, 'I have
to work on something but I don't feel like it. I'm
angry.' 'And what about Aldo?' 'He's angry too, he
wants to sleep, he doesn't want to work.' 'Giovanni?'
'Oh, he doesn't care. He's happy. He knows I'll do
everything anyway.' 'Giacomo?' 'He's stressed. He
says it's going to be a disaster. The book. He says
I'll mess up at the readings.' 'Eh, he's just the
anxious type.' 'Poor thing. You can handle Giacomo.'
'All right. I have to go, the screening is about to
start.'

13 January, I'm in Milan.
   It's night. 'I'm going to bed. AGG are tired' (we
will often call them that, Aldo-Giovanni-Giacomo:
AGG). 'Did you eat?' 'No.' 'Come on, don't starve the
poor babies.' 'In 13 minutes it's my day. Publication
day!' I'm so excited. 'Yes! Good luck!' 'I'm scared to
do the interviews.' 'Have Aldo do them. Aldo is good
at them.' 'But he's sleeping. Like always. He takes
after you.'

14 January, in Milan. Publication day.
   A thousand messages: 'Did you hear the interview
on the radio? How'd it go?' 'Yes, all good.' 'We're going
to have to figure out how to handle everything and
AGG. If we get nominated for the Strega Prize ... Will

we?' 'Definitely.' 'But how will I manage it, I'll be big as a balloon in July' (or even bigger, probably, if everything goes well; I don't say that I would have already had to give birth, with this pregnancy we're pretending isn't so complicated). 'You'll be so cool, pregnant for the Strega.'

(smash everything, smash everything)

And I picture myself there, at the Strega ceremony in July, very pregnant and glowing.

(bash, bash my head in)

I do readings online, interviews, one at a bookstore, but still streaming. Everyone tells me: your energy is insane. AGG giggle.

It goes like this, then a nosedive into darkness. Fight after fight with Andrea. I yell that I'm the one in this situation. That I'm the one who won't be able to work like before, that I won't be able to promote my book. That he's doing everything he has to do without any of the problems I have even now. That I'm going nuts while he's perfectly fine. He says: 'You wanted this so badly, didn't you?'

(he replied and would reply many other times: You wanted this so badly, didn't you?)

(I said and would say many other times: It's not just my thing, don't you get that?)

*

(he said and would say many other times: It's not just
your thing, don't you get that?)

(I don't think we get each other)

He says: 'I'm looking for a house. We have to move.
We can't stay here, in a sixth-floor walk-up without at
least one more bedroom.'
    That puts me over the moon.

When he goes on set, sometimes I don't hear from him
the entire day.
    When he goes on set, sometimes he leaves sweet
messages for the four of us. I still have those messages,
but I don't know where they are any more and I don't
want to know.

Today, 3 January 2022, I have to reconsider this book. I said I started writing it still in the grip of an absurd black hope. I wrote that this book is affecting me.

Maybe it isn't any more.

Or rather, the truth is it never did. It's all bullshit. Just coincidences taken as signs.

I'm just looking for something. Something to believe.

I'm writing what happened, but not what's happening now. What will happen tomorrow, I can't know. But what is happening now, I can't write. This isn't a diary, I can't write every day while everything is going on. I don't have the strength. Or the will.

Something happened today that made me rethink this book. Something that once again erodes my futile insistence on giving this story a happy ending. I've never written books with happy endings. I've written books with dark endings, open endings, hopeful endings, but never happy endings.

I really want to be able to write one, know how to write one, one day.

I have to rethink happy endings altogether.

I have to rethink what I remember. I need help – medical records, texts, emails – to remember.

I've omitted messages where Andrea and I are having a big fight or saying awful things to each other. I've omitted that one time he mentioned two children, and I said, What about the third? Did you forget him? And it makes me so mad, but in the end, what am I actually hoping for?

For example, we fight a lot because he says he might not be able to come to Milan in a month, he has a shoot. And I say, fuck's sake, it's not like you're with someone who doesn't put work first, someone who doesn't understand what work means to you (and to me). I've done everything alone. I went to Milan to get lectured about death, alone. But this time you have to come. Your signature is needed for the procedure. And you're needed too.

He knows this time he has no choice. He starts trying to work out how he can be away from the set for three days – and not one more.

I'm writing about the past, it's true, but I'm writing it today. Those fights aren't important now. And not because I've forgiven him, or because they seem stupid, or because I feel like I'm the innocent victim and he's the villain. The reality is more nuanced. It's that there's always a focus to every story you tell. Whether it's made up or whether it's true. A focus like the lens on a video camera or on an iPhone. You can't capture everything. You decide what your focus is and home in on it. My focus is the three of them.

If he were a fictional character, Andrea would change over the course of his journey from A to B to C. In real life, he's more like a Covid transmission chart, an electrocardiogram, or a child's drawing. Up and down, changing and turning back, spiralling inwards, repeating, flip-flopping. In a novel, in a fictional story, a character should never repeat themselves. Andrea is

repetitive, he unloads and goes back and forth errat-
ically, without any kind of helpful pattern. I'm no
different, my hypothetical graph would be completely
chaotic. The only ones who head straight down their
path, towards their fate, are those three.

Yesterday, Andrea told me again that I have to get past this whole thing. He says it when we have a big fight. He said it at Christmas when we didn't have anything to do and he suggested watching *Harry Potter* and I replied, 'We watched that last year, I can't.' He says it when I don't know how to get somewhere in Rome and he tells me to take the scooter and I say I'm pissed off with the scooter, I'm not taking that thing any more. He said it yesterday when we had a fight and I said, 'Ugh, I just need a distraction, I don't want to think about what we were doing last Christmas.' When he says it I take my head and throw it across the room so I can't hear him any more.

What else can I do?

Men – I'm told – men don't understand, they can't. Men. Bah. I don't know what I think of men. I don't know what I think of women. Often I don't know what I think, and I don't want to know.

Until the end of the first trimester, this being a medically assisted pregnancy, I have to continue the injections and all the other medication.

I take folic acid, Progynova (2 in the morning, 2 in the evening), low-dose aspirin, Estraderm patches (2 every 48 hours), Prednisone, Pleyris injections (2 a day).

I can't wait to get past the first trimester and have a normal pregnancy (which is crazy, since that's a phrase that in this pregnancy does not exist).

My book comes out, I do readings, I do interviews. I have a month not to think about my children not being born, about one almost certainly not being born.

There's a room in my house that I hate. It's the office, which faces north and is always freezing. I never use it. I'm always in the living room, which gets lots of sun. That month, as so often, I spend a lot of time alone. Or alone in a manner of speaking. It's funny, even when I'm alone there are four of us.

We're on lockdown, there's a curfew. Andrea's on set with a permit to shoot until late. He can see the night-time that we, the rest of Italy, can't see any more.

I spend a lot of time alone, and I torture myself with the fear that my pregnancy will be bad for the book. I haven't changed, I'm still me. And then I feel elated and tell myself that this pregnancy can only help the book. I haven't changed, I'm still me.

Andrea fades away.

I stay curled up at home and often I feel alone and afraid. Many other times I feel happy.

When Andrea is out, I do the readings and interviews in the living room, which is filled with light.

When Andrea is home, I hole up in the office, in the cold, because I'm embarrassed to speak in front of him. In time, I will come to love that room.

Every time I present the book, someone asks if I have kids, since the novel talks about a mother who has a very difficult relationship with her small children. Since it talks about, in a word, motherhood.

I hadn't thought of it at all when I wrote the book. But now the questions come, and there are four of us. And I say I don't have children, but inside I'm gleeful: Al, Joe and Jack tell me, Whoa, you're a good actor. Or they say, Whoa, you're such a liar. Or they swim around, they kick, and every week, every day, every minute, whoa, do they grow.

(I will keep on promoting the book for a long time after everything happens; people will keep on asking me, do you have kids? And I'll have to answer, and I'll have to tell my brain, respond, but don't think; respond, but don't cry; I will never cry, ever, for the world to see, not even when everything happens; are you sure you can keep doing these events? they ask me. I'm sure, I'm sure as always. You don't need to fight yourself all the time, Antonella, those who know me best will say. Ah, but I do. I thrive on combat. On battles for or against me.)

At the end of January, my publisher's publicity department sends me the entry form for the Strega Prize. I sign a document stating that if selected I will be available to go on the prize tour. I sign and my body splits in two: one half says it'll be fine, the other half says, if you do get this, by the time the Strega tour comes around you'll be stuck in bed. Shut up, head. When has a head ever spoken and had a point.

Before readings I go to the Ivorian hairdresser down from my apartment. She washes and blow-dries my hair. I sit there, with her, and with the other three. I feel like she knows. Even though no one knows. I feel like everyone knows even though no one knows.

(Afterwards, I'll have to go back to her. I'll last a few months. Then, I'll change hairdressers. I can't go into that salon any more.)

It's a perfect month. Early January to early February.
  Thanks for this time, novel.
  Thanks for this time, Al, Joe and Jack.

'What are you doing today?' I write to Giulia. 'I'm at home with the kids, working, do you want to come by? We could eat together.' 'Sure. I'm going to Milan on

Sunday. I don't know if I'll come back with two, one, or none.' 'You'll come back with the right number, I'm sure.' Pause, then, 'Shit, how is it Sunday.' 'Yep.' I pause. 'So I'm going to do some book stuff and then I'll come over, OK?' Is life what happens while you're busy warding off fear? Or is it all the moments of joy and oblivion you manage to carve out so it doesn't take hold of you?

I go to Giulia's. I have a phone interview to do, so I lock myself in the kids' room. I remember that interview very well. By the time it comes out, everything has happened. I remember being locked in that room with its cribs and toys. I remember the grey, late January sky. I remember the rooftops of Rome from the window of Giulia's sixth-floor apartment in Furio Camillo. I remember answering the questions, while everything, everything is coated with some sticky substance whose colour I can't discern, this sticky substance which is the awareness that the three of them are there, and it never leaves me.

I remember we order Chinese. That I eat, but not much. I remember Giulia's partner coming home and being particularly kind to me. I remember us laughing, Giulia and I, as we eat. No mention of Sunday, when I'll leave for the hospital in Milan. I don't know if Giulia or her partner are thinking about that. I know I'm not.

I also worry about whether Al, Joe and Jack like Chinese food.

I smoke a cigarette.

On Saturday, I take a walk around the city with Carlo. It's sunny out.

It's 30 January. We go into a church near Regina Coeli, I don't remember which. There's a sign on the church door: 'Do not bang on your way out.' Carlo takes a picture of me peeking outside the door cautiously, mask on, with this big sign next to me 'Do not bang on your way out.' I post it on Instagram and the comments are laughs, and I don't even know what sort of secret message I've just sent out into the universe.

It's the last picture I have with them in Rome. But it's not the last good memory yet.

We get to Milan on Sunday evening. The operation is scheduled for Tuesday. On Tuesday I'll be twelve weeks and two days. That's a lot of time with the three of them. Giulia: 'I'm sure that starting Wednesday the situation will become more normal, at least. Still hard, of course, but manageable.' 'OK, but no one is thinking about what I'm about to face, right now' (at this point I'm resentful and whiny, and I'm lashing out at Giulia but being passive-aggressive about it; I want people to feel bad for me so I play the victim) 'like it's no big deal. I mean, I don't even know if it's going to hurt. How I'll be afterwards. How they'll be. Who knows? And just because I don't ask for sympathy and act tough' (this again). 'Well, if it makes you feel any better, I'm thinking about it.'

A few hours later she texts me, 'Send me the link to the hotel so I know where to picture you.'

Rereading this message now makes me cry. That she wanted to picture me where I was.

I said that writing this book doesn't affect me any more. That it never affected me; I imagined it. That's not true (it's true, it's not true). It's only in the moments when I'm writing that I don't think about this unacceptable present.

In those moments, even immersed in pain and memories I don't want to remember, there's an undercurrent of joy. Because I'm writing my book.

After everything that has abandoned me, this remains. This persistence. It's not about salvation. It's not about redemption. It's not about urgency, or necessity. It's about trying to create something that still means something to me, to try with everything I've got. Because ultimately, it's about existing.

A few days before I have to leave for Milan, I go on a walk with a friend. Via Urbana, Via Leonina, Via della Madonna dei Monti, Via Tor de' Conti, Largo Corrado Ricci, Via dei Fori Imperiali.

There's no one around. It's Covid. I think the walk is against regulations but I don't really remember which one or why. My friend, who's thirty, tells me about flirtations, dates, sex, underground parties. She asks me for advice. She laughs. She has platinum blond hair, green eyes, smooth skin. I feel old, and heavy with these three babies inside, as if I'd eaten too much. I think I'm not attractive in her eyes, not attractive to anyone – from the inside, let alone from the outside. I think how much I wish I had sex, flirtations, and parties to talk about. I feel like I'm taking it from all sides, and not in the fun way. All I have is endless medical terminology, monochorionic triamniotic pregnancy, belly injections – menotropin, hCG – Estraderm patches – I've put one on my belly every 48 hours for longer than I can remember, they're irritating, they're itchy; all I have is cortisone, because I have an underactive thyroid which could cause miscarriage, progesterone suppositories, and Progynova pills; I don't even feel like having a Bloody Mary, not even at aperitivo hour. I walk along and I say to myself, why aren't I like other mothers? Happy, happy, happy, sleeping the afternoon sleep of the righteous. If this were a normal pregnancy, I would have these same thoughts. Because when it comes down to it, I'm a shitty mother. Or not a mother at all.

At Piazza Venezia she says to me, 'And what about you? What's going on in your life?'

I want to take a trip around the world to Mexico America Panama Brazil Tierra del Fuego the Bahamas Mauritius Australia Melbourne New Zealand, I want to swim in the ocean, dance all night to reggaeton in Cuba drinking rum, drinking coconut milk, piña coladas, breathing in the Caribbean air, saying wow, I've never seen anything like this.

'Let's do it!' she replies, all excited.

'Yes!' I say.

Hey – the triplets say.

What – I reply.

Hey – they say again.

My first night in Milan there's a curfew and restaurants close at 6 p.m. The only place to have dinner is the hotel. It's not a nice hotel, just the closest one to the clinic. I argue with a tan-faced waiter because his mask is under his nose and he talks too close to Andrea. He talks a lot. Andrea is too polite to tell him to get lost. I'm not.

We feel pretty good.

We are completely oblivious.

We chat about the awful food – I can't stomach any of it, even just reading the items on the menu puts the smells in my head and makes me nauseous – and about Al, Joe and Jack.

Joe won't accept anything less than a Michelin-star restaurant. He'll have to get over that.

The night is oblivious.

We wake up early the next morning, oblivious.

We go to the hospital.

We walk there, it's just a few minutes away, past some roadworks. Masks are mandatory outdoors. We are completely oblivious to what's happening. It's like we're on a day trip.

The hospital is reassuring. Everyone is very nice. Andrea has to wait in the hallway outside the ward – what a horrible name, Obstetric Pathology (you know, one of those names you see and think will never apply to you). I go in, they have me fill out some forms, they ask for my blood type for tomorrow's procedure. I don't know my blood type. The receptionist says, 'How do you not know, it's essential in pregnancy.' But I've never had all the other tests that other women do at this part of a pregnancy. That scares me. Why don't I have to take the tests that other expecting mothers do? Reason answers that in my situation it's a matter of life or death, that there's no point in having tests on three babies who might die (but I quell this rational voice when it comes, and I never mention it to Andrea, who obviously has no idea how strange it is not to have us listen to the heartbeat, not to have these tests done, and I continue letting rational thoughts pass right through me, as if I were made of water, or air, or nothing, holding fast to the magical thinking that says if you really want something, *really* want it, it'll come true; which means if it doesn't it will be the fault of my monstrous half . . .). 'Is there anyone you can ask?' 'What?' 'Your blood type.' 'Only my mother. But my mother doesn't know, she doesn't even know I'm here, she has no idea about what's going on, and . . .' 'All right.' The receptionist smiles and seems to understand. 'We'll just take a quick sample now.'

Thank you.

I go to the waiting room. When they call me I can let Andrea know to meet us in the room with the doctors I saw last month. Andrea is constantly outside on the phone because he's not on set but has to carry on as if he were. I chat about the novel with my editor as if I weren't here on the border between life and death but cosy at home, then I chat with friends who don't know, making up where I've gone and why, and then I chat with Andrea.

The exam room is very big. All dark, to see the ultrasound better. They're extremely kind. Andrea is . . . freaked out? I don't know what the adj-

(Today, 5 January 2022, I'm thinking: since this is too difficult a moment to talk about, maybe instead of stopping for two hours to stare at the wall, out of the window, at Instagram, Facebook, Twitter, or to read pointless news, or smoke another cigarette – an IQOS and a regular cigarette, to be precise, as the smell of smoke gives me a headache; instead of pushing the ashtray away thinking that'll keep the smell away, thinking, what is there to eat? All I want is to eat, getting up, looking around, there's nothing to eat, plus I have an excruciating headache, and so I'm nauseous too, but it's not the right nausea; instead of texting someone, instead of looking at happy and/or sad pictures – anything but the ones I need for this book – instead of moving, sitting on the couch with my legs folded and computer on my lap, or at the desk with the computer on the tabletop, instead of thinking I'm going blind, I can't see any more, instead of thinking no matter what I'll never wear glasses, instead of putting together a playlist to write this book to – this is a book I can't write in silence, but for now the only soundtrack that works is *Lost*, because it's calming, but I've got so sick of it by now – instead of all this, maybe could you try to shield yourself with writing? Write this part in verse? Only write short sentences, without adjectives? Or skip ahead to the aftermath? Take a risk and write without vowels? Think of the stylistic innovation of writing without vowels. Or, I don't know, write only in dialogue? Without description. Worth a try. But first, finish the word 'adjective.' OK.)

-ective.

No, hold on (I'm a coward).

Yesterday, 4 January 2022, I watched Darren Aronofsky's *Mother!* It's part of my shock therapy, starting with the title. Not exactly a title that appeals to me right now. At this point Andrea doesn't even ask me 'can you handle it?' any more because I've said a million times that I can handle anything just fine (total lie). That nothing gets to me (after all, it's been months, *you have to get past it*, is what he would say if I told him I couldn't handle it. I don't want him to tell me that again. Because otherwise, since he's the only witness to the crime, I'd have to kill him. And not because he witnessed the crime – which was also his – but because if he really meant for me to take that phrase 'now you have to get past this' to heart, I'd have to take a knife and slit his throat. Though it wouldn't be in my best interests. I'm too old. Who else could I try to have another child with then?). Sitting on the couch, watching this movie – my pick – I don't stop squirming for a second, and this time not because it's a horror movie (I'm scared of horror movies too) but because I'm anticipating the moment when my heart falls to pieces. In reality, it was shattered from the start, it's a movie called *Mother* . . . what did I expect?

But I have to watch. I have to show myself that I can handle it.

It's Jennifer Lawrence, with her perfect tits, her every pore emanating youth, passionately in love with a poet, Javier Bardem, who's going through a crisis that's bigger than her. Now, when I see young women out in the world, I no longer see them as young women. I see them as pregnancies waiting to happen. A concentration of hormones, ripe like figs about to split open and ooze milky sap, an engorged ball of hormones ready to explode into a billion babies at the slightest touch. The opposite of me, who . . .

I don't want to go over the entire movie, but forgive me for the spoilers. At a certain point, Bardem is finally able to start writing again. I identified with him the whole time. The desperation you feel when you can't write. The fear. And I felt sorry for her the whole time – ultimately, she has nothing else in life, all she wants is a child (I said to myself: I'm not like that, I've never been like that).

Then when she gets pregnant, I couldn't take it any more. I hated her. I hated her the morning after they have sex – incredible sex, the kind I don't even remember, when you're not thinking about whether you're ovulating (then keeping your legs in the air to help the sperm swim up inside, not getting up right away so they don't fall out, a bunch of bullshit I always knew to be untrue but did anyway, of course; but not any more) – I hated her when she wakes up in the morning and says to her husband, 'I'm pregnant.' Ugh, that sanctimonious face. Like a woman who has it all figured out. Who the day after a single fuck with her husband is pregnant. And knows it. I hated the smile she gives him as she tells him. I envied her as if she were a real person, and this a real story. That bitch.

Then there's a transitional part I won't get into. But this prospective baby brings fecundity to his work as well. His book comes out and it's a triumph. The critics love it. The fans love it. He was dead, and now he's alive again. Yet she doesn't want him to go out into the world to enjoy the fruit of all that labour. She tells him: stay here, it's just you and me.

'What the fuck is wrong with you!' I yell at the TV. 'What is wrong with her,' I say to Andrea.

Then there's a scene where they're standing face to face outside the house. She's ready to pop, her belly is huge, while fans are calling his name (how happy he must be, finally reaching that level of success – total happiness).

And my head started spinning. Holy shit. I'm him *and* her. I'm Bardem and his ambition. I'm Jennifer Lawrence and her laser focus on that baby.

A young, fair woman vs. an older, taller, swarthier man. It was like seeing myself double. My opposing parts facing off. Each wanting to destroy the other.

And I felt stupid, to be a woman.

Then I thought: is that how Andrea sees me? Like that woman?

I rarely speak with the doctor at the Y clinic. But she's the one who prescribed the medications I'm supposed to take until the end of the first trimester.

The third month ends on 31 January. Week twelve. In another pregnancy, I'd almost be in the clear. Most miscarriages happen within the first twelve weeks. On 29 January, I wrote a message to the Y doctor. I summarised my treatment thus far and asked how to proceed.

She wrote instructions on a piece of paper and sent me the photo on WhatsApp. So I'm supposed to work it all out, right?

Here it is, exactly, down to the bold and bullet points:

Sig.ra Lattanzi
determine with regular ob-gyn when to stop folic acid and aspirin

Week 12:
- Stop estraderm
- 2 progynova morn + 2 progynova eve
- ½ tab prednisone
- 3 supp (200 mg, vaginal) progesterone, morn, noon, eve

Week 13:
- 1 progynova morn + 2 eve
- Stop prednisone
- 1 progesterone morn and 1 eve

Week 14:

- 2 progynova eve
- 1 progesterone eve

Week 15:

- 1 progynova eve
- Stop progesterone

Week 16 stop treatment

I thanked her, feeling good, and replied OK, as if I didn't have this procedure coming up on 2 February, four days away. As if, OK, let's taper down these medications and wrap up this weird part. From now on, it'll be just a regular pregnancy.

I checked the calendar on my iPhone from last year to remember the dates. It's still there, the train ticket: *31 January 2021, Roma Termini–Milano Centrale, Frecciarossa 9548, carr. 7, posti 5B, 9B* (Andrea is always happy when our seats aren't together, that way I don't bug him by chatting the whole time), *PNR M2Z7AN.*

I hadn't looked at it since. God, I hate you so much, last-year Toni.

When I get to Milan on the 31st, I've just started to taper down my fertility drugs. I don't put those itchy patches on my belly any more. How I will mourn them. I'll never finish the treatment plan the Y doctor sent.

I go back into the big, dark room (sorry, I have to catch my breath, I've lost my nerve).

I lie back on the exam table and open my legs. Beside me, the ultrasound machine and the doctors. Across from me, a big wall monitor displaying the ultrasound. Where is Andrea? I don't remember him. If I squint I find him, beside me on the right. But I don't remember him. The doctor in charge of the ultrasound pats my bent leg. Just for a second. I want to cry. I don't. I've cried enough. Enough crying.

She slides the probe over my belly. I see them. On the screen, three babies at 12 weeks, 4 days. They're moving a lot. The doctor points, 'Here's the first, here's the second, here's the third.' She smiles. 'Here are the hands, here are the feet, here is the head.'

'How are they doing?'

They're all good, they're great, all three. No one would've thought we'd lose even one along the way. I'm torn. My bones are broken inside. They made, and still make, noise. Half of me wants all of them to thrive, and heaves a sigh of relief every time that miracle occurs (everyone said that the possibility of all three of them making it was extremely low, even lower than the perennially low tide in Sabaudia). The other half wants one, or two, to reabsorb spontaneously – be honest, for god's sake, you mean, to die – so that it could become a twin or single pregnancy, still difficult but doable. A normal pregnancy.

(You're so dramatic, always all or nothing, Andrea has told me a million times, and Giulia has told me a million times; it's true, I'm stubborn, intense, I always want everything and more, but this time I wanted something I've never wanted in my whole life: to be able to combine the word 'me' with the word 'normal'. My friends love me for my quirks. You're crazy, they always say. You're weird, they always say. I act like it's funny; as a kid it was fun being weird. Now it's not fun any more. You know that woman my age with matching earrings and necklace and perfect hair, in a classy outfit with the bag to match? I want that to be me.)

They're all doing great and I'm the devil and the angel and I'm elated and enraged. Why are you putting your siblings' lives in danger? Why didn't one or two of you just vanish on your own? These are not motherly thoughts. These are not thoughts one would share. I want all of them to live and thrive. But here I am bound to honesty, so.

They keep moving and the gynaecologist pushes my belly a little to shift them. Now I can see Andrea on my right, I remember Andrea and me saying look! and he looks, and the doctor, as if this were just another pregnancy says, look. And then, as she silently takes their measurements and murmurs to her colleagues, she says, in a flat tone as if saying today, tomorrow, in passing, 'They're females.'

I had always thought of them as boys. I was certain. Yet this whole time they were girls. I never knew the sex of the children I didn't have. I didn't ask. They didn't say. But these, these are girls. And now I know their sex, they're irrefutably here. They're not foetuses, they're not shadows on a screen, they're not Al, Joe and Jack. They are my three daughters. I think: my mother will be happy that they're girls. My sister too. They always liked girls. Three identical girls who— I saw in the monochorionic-diamniotic pregnancy group I'm in—at first even their mothers can't tell apart ('Mamas, what do I do, put different coloured bracelets on them?' and they laugh in the comments). Three daughters. My three baby girls.

Three daughters with the same eyes, same ears, same hair, same hands, same feet, same face, same height. Three girls that are almost disturbing to see all identical, as if they were clones, three girls who will say, 'Daddy!' 'Daddy!' 'Daddy!'

They're my three daughters. They're real. They're alive. And I'm their mother.

The room explodes into a thousand streamers of boundless joy that has no place here. I hate the world, because it doesn't want me to be happy. Because it doesn't make sense to be happy. And despite everything I am happy and Andrea is happy and there are three girls and they are ours and we're going to have three babies. Now it's certain.

In passing, we see a face. A fleeting morphology — the scan that photographs a baby as it is, an actual photograph — for an instant we see one of their faces. Nose, eyes, mouth. In the photo she looks yellow. And then she disappears. The doctor doesn't say, this is the morphological scan. I recognise it because I'm a woman and I've seen the morphological scans of friends. It's the moment when we say: look at that little nose. Who do they look like?

It goes by in a flash. The only copy I have of this photo is here, in my mind. I never got one. They never gave it to me. Later, I'll say to Andrea: Did you see that yellow picture? Like going from black and white cinema to colour. From silent to sound.

Who were you? The only daughter whose face I saw. Who were you? Who were you to become?

'I can't write,' I tell Andrea today. It's 27 January. It took me nearly a month to work up the courage to write this part of the book. I don't want to write. 'Can't you write it?'

'As myself?' he says.

'You know the story.'

'You want to co-write it?' He laughs. 'A novel *à quatre mains*?'

I think: *quatre* ... four, six, eight, ten (I'm not good at calculations, as I've said – I have to count) hands. A tentet. A book by ten hands.

In a flash, I see her. My daughter.

Mouth, nose, forehead, eyes, chin. All yellow and a little strange, as morphology scans always look. Otherworldly. I see her for an instant. One of them. Which one is she?

'All three girls are doing great.'

It's the first time someone refers to them as girls.

And the heartbeat. This time, their three hearts resound throughout the room. Beating very very fast. A sound that could drive you mad. A sound that's immediately addictive, that you want to hear on and on.

You see them, itty bitty blue and red, on the monitor, pulsing. Living things. You see the lines rise and fall like my mother's moods when we were little, like my own moods for as long as I can recall. But this up and down isn't anything strange – it's life.

Heart, hand, face, look, yes, I'm looking, look, all three girls are doing great.

And instead of being happy, somehow we must feel sad, even now. I had forgotten, for a moment, that we are here to *reduce* one of them. That we left the hotel as five but won't be returning as five. Somehow, we have to be sad again. We waited all the way to 12 weeks, 4 days for the procedure because that's the last possible day to abort. This past month, the doctors had explained euphemistically, we were supposed to hope that one or two of them *wouldn't make it* on their own. And if one of the three, at this scan on this advanced date, showed signs of any kind of problem, we would have to decide: *reduce* this one, or these two. Because they won't make it anyway.

But we have three beautiful, growing, healthy baby girls. They are ours. They are here with us, all three doing so well that the gynaecologist asks me if I used donor eggs – that is, if the eggs didn't come from me, but a younger woman – because judging by their features, they appear to be from younger eggs.

'Antonella, are you sure the eggs were your own? It's important for the procedure. Naturally, some women feel embarrassed . . .'

Yes. They're mine. The eggs and the daughters.

The numbers look good. Everything looks good. When we leave the hospital tomorrow after this operation, at least one of the three will be gone. At least I don't have to decide which. I wish I could say goodbye to one of these girls. But it's impossible. I can't. I don't want to. Not even now, as I write, do I want to. I don't think, Goodbye. I think, See you soon. And then I laugh: Soon? All three of you – when I leave this room, this hospital, whatever I do, you're always with me.

We're having three baby girls, I thought before, convinced.

Even now I think so, as we walk out. Andrea and I play around with the numbers but numbers are meaningless. One, two, three: the maths fall apart in our delusional minds. We don't understand what we've come here for. We don't understand what we're going to do tomorrow.

*

We go for coffee, for breakfast, filled with joy. How can we be so out of touch? I write to Giulia: 'They're girls, they're doing great!' I write in my chat with Bianca and Ada: 'They're girls, they're doing great!'

'Girls! OMG, girls!' they reply, with hearts and emojis and cheers and how amazing and how exciting in the chat.

I write to Dr S.: 'Good morning, Dr S. We're just leaving the hospital. They're girls ...' Next line: 'All three of them are doing great.' Next line: 'The procedure is tomorrow.' Next line: 'I'll take a picture of the report and send it to you.' This is what we always do. Whenever I have a test or scan somewhere else, I take a picture and send it to him. He calls me back right away, with his fatherly voice. He sends his encouragement, saying that everything is going to be fine, and then I say: 'I'll send you the report now.' And he says: 'No need. We'll talk tomorrow.' That throws me off a little. Why doesn't he want to see my three babies?

Once we had finished and left the ultrasound room, the doctors repeated all the risks to us (though this is the first time Andrea is hearing them in person) – the risks if we choose to keep all three (once, when I was very young, my best friend, a girlfriend, died. That day, someone said to me, 'Entrust her to God.' The doctors don't say that, of course. But if I were to choose to keep all three I would be entrusting myself to God. I'm not the sort of person, though, who can entrust myself to another). The risks of the procedure: 40 per cent chance of success. The risks if the operation goes well and two survive. Never-ending risks, at every moment, up to birth and even after.

We hear them but we're out of our minds and don't understand.

'Are you ready?'

'We're ready.'

'Then we'll see you tomorrow. Now go and try to take your mind off it.'

They don't have to tell us twice. Regardless, we have no clue what's actually happening.

1 February 2021. 2.48 p.m. The same day as the above events, a few hours later.

In my chat with Bianca and Ada, Bianca begins a text with this: 'I would like to nominate Antonella Lattanzi's *Questo giorno che incombe* for the Strega Prize.'

I know it's hard to believe, but the same day I find out that my babies are girls, the Strega committee announces the first candidates for the prize. And in that first round is me.

I'm flooded with messages from friends, writers, editors. The announcement is all over the internet. I'm walking through Milan, right after my appointment, and I can't explain how happy I am, euphoric, to have seen those babies, and happy about this news. I call my mother and say, 'Mamma, did you see? We're up for the Strega!' I tell her that it's a lengthy process, and this nomination is only the first step. I tell her to wait before soaring up to cloud nine (I think of *Neverending Story*: 'Bastian, you're old enough to get your head out of the clouds and start keeping both feet on the ground.' But I don't want to!). I walk down Via Dante, a huge street, with Piazza Castello straight ahead; most museums are closed due to Covid, so we stroll through the castle gardens, we walk all around this big city, and I'm loving it, walking on air.

I don't tell my mother anything about the babies. I don't tell the publisher anything. I answer emails, phone calls, texts. We're exhilarated. I say: it's a sign. Everything is a sign.

Anything can be a sign when you want it to be.

We have a good time that day. We wander all of Milan, without stopping. We don't give a thought to what's going to happen tomorrow.

I have a risotto alla milanese, Andrea ossobuco, which he loves. We're the first visitors at a small museum that has just reopened after Covid restrictions.

In the evening, we return to the hotel.

We have a drink. I have a glass of prosecco (or two).

We're completely out of our minds.

'What are we going to name them?' I say.

I think he's going to reply, what are you talking about, it's too soon, tomorrow we have to ... But instead ...

'You pick one, I'll pick the other. We have two, after all. OK?' (two, we say, as if nothing were going on; we have no idea what we're saying.)

'OK.'

Me: 'I want to call her Annalena Angela.' A second name, after my mother.

Him: 'Mine is Bianca Cristina.' The second name, after his mother.

I say: 'It's a deal.'

He says: 'It's a deal.'

We toast our two daughters. Annalena and Bianca.

'But there's a problem,' I add, solemn.

Another problem? 'What?' he asks, on edge.

'You know how they pronounce the name Annalena

in Bari? It's like, Anna-LEH-na.' I tighten the vowel and exaggerate the cadence.

'Anna-LEH-na,' he repeats, laughing, imitating my accent badly. 'What's wrong with that?'

We don't even think about how, the next day, at least one of them will be gone.

The next day, we're afraid.

I pull out the ultrasound pictures and tell Andrea: 'Look. This is the last time you'll be seeing one of them.'

He says, 'Stop.'

We walk past the roadworks towards the hospital. We don't speak.

Just like yesterday, only I am allowed in the waiting room. They have me fill out a form that details everything that could possibly happen.

Andrea texts me the whole time. 'What are you doing? Are you waiting?' 'Yes.' All around me, pregnant women, with round bellies. I'm one of you, and I am very proud. For the first time, I don't envy you.

Looking for a distraction, I scroll through Facebook. I even make a dumb post, something about manicures and nail polish (how I hate that post, how I hate myself at that moment, how much I hate that nth diversionary post. It feels like an insult. It feels like an act of hubris). Last night I had another dream about pregnancy ruining my work. I woke up in a terrible mood. What do you think other pregnant woman dream about? I ask myself.

They call me in. They have me undress. I text Andrea: 'I'm going in.' He can't be with me during the operation, but as soon as it's finished they'll call him in.

You're a woman, and you have to do everything

alone. The body containing these little girls is yours. Accept it.

They put me on a gurney in a hospital gown. It won't be total anaesthesia, just sedation. How much Xanax can I get? I take it already, when I'm going through a rough patch, but it never does anything. I want all the Xanax there is. They give it to me. There are interns observing the procedure. They're young, and they talk and laugh and one of them has curly blonde hair and another one is pregnant and I hate all of them.

I wait on that gurney for a century. The Xanax does nothing. A doctor I've never met will be doing the operation, but the doctor I saw here last month will be with me. She tries to make me smile. Distract me.

They take me into a room. It's not an operating room. This is a life-and-death operation, but it's an out-patient procedure. Afterwards, I only have to stay a couple of hours for observation. To see how the babies – the foetuses – react to the reduction. Then I can go to my hotel, wait overnight to see how they are. If they're all right, I can return to Rome. The death of the remaining foetuses would usually happen within 72 hours, they said. After that, I go on with the rest of the pregnancy – still very difficult, but less so.

But those are just words.

It's sunny in Milan. On the way in, we see scores of pregnant women and couples with newborns in prams entering and leaving the hospital. Several prams are double. I stare at them, mesmerised. I look and think of when that will be me. I can't wait.

I don't say anything to Andrea. But he notices the prams, smiles at me and says, 'Look at all the different double prams. We'll have to figure out which one is the best.'

It's so sunny. Can you, who are reading this, believe that I remember this as a dazzling moment? A kind of incredible we, us.

Now they take me in for the operation.

Covid tests are just like pregnancy tests.

I go to Spain for work, 18–23 January 2022.

It's the peak of the Omicron variant.

To enter Spain, you don't need to take a rapid test. To enter Italy, you do. I have to test before returning, and if I'm positive I'll have to stay and quarantine in Spain.

I have reason to worry that the test will be positive. I've been with a close friend who met me there to spend some time together. We had a very nice few days. A nurse comes to our hotel to administer the test the night before our return flight to Rome. She gives us the tests. She sets them on the table. Just like a pregnancy test, one red line appears first to indicate that the test was done correctly. If a second line appears, the result is positive.

We wait, on tenterhooks. First line. Test is valid. After taking a million pregnancy tests, I know that when it's positive the second line appears right away. Seconds pass without a second line. I already know they're negative.

I tell my friend, 'If it hasn't appeared by now, it's not going to. It's like a pregnancy test.'

The sentence just came out of my mouth, even though it's something I never want to talk about. If you don't say it, it doesn't exist. I don't know what my friend makes of this sentence. But she doesn't say anything, for my benefit I'm sure.

We look at the tests.

Who knows what my mind is thinking. Who knows what my body is saying. For months and months, for years, I've been constantly taking tests. Some I want to be positive (pregnancy) and others (Covid) I want to be negative. I've come to think that if you hope for a positive it'll definitely turn out negative and vice versa. In those seconds I hope for nothing. So fate won't hear me. The test is negative. The second line doesn't appear.

I'm not pregnant.

Ah, no – I don't have Covid.

And so I'm relieved, we hug, I'm happy not to have Covid and not to have to quarantine, alone, in a hotel in Spain, while my mind – which is much more elementary – asks me: Well? Which is it? What am I supposed to hope for? Positive or negative?

It's 27 January 2022. Again. I don't want to explain the reasons now, but the last few months have been very difficult in terms of this story. I don't want to explain why and I won't – this isn't a diary – but Coronavirus again entered the picture; I had to avoid it and spent the holidays holed up at home, once again spiraling in a vortex of fertility clinics, treatments, injections and frustrations ('You can't go anywhere, you'll risk getting Covid, you have to focus on this,' Giulia told me sternly over Christmas. I responded, 'Well what if I focus only on this and it still goes wrong?' There you go). On 31 December, after yet another unsuccessful attempt, the gynaecologist gives me a shot of a medicine called Gonasi. It's used to trigger follicle rupture. He prescribes sex on 1, 2 and 3 January. This whole time, Andrea and I are fighting. Imagine a day when you've spent every minute fighting with your partner, you hate him, and he's spent every minute fighting with you, he hates you, and then it comes time to have sex, fuck, whatever you want to call it. *You have to.* Imagine what that's like.

We do it. What can we do. This is us now.

Rather, we do it two of the three days. On the third, we can't handle it. I go to the bedroom. He sleeps on the sofa. This is how it is. Like this, or the other way around.

On 9 January, I take a Clearblue test. This one doesn't have lines. It's large print, PREGNANT / NOT PREGNANT.

As I've learned, I hope for nothing while I wait. I do other things, answer messages, tidy up the house (something I never do). Then, it appears: PREGNANT. I still believe in that miracle that friends, acquaintances and internet forums have told me about: 'It will happen naturally when you least expect it.' Though this is not exactly natural. I've had ovarian stimulation and a Gonasi shot, which is chorionic gonadotropin, i.e. the pregnancy hormone, used to make ovulation happen at a certain time. In that moment, though, I do not know that Gonasi contains the pregnancy hormone. I write to Giulia, 'I know it's too early, but' and send her a picture of the test saying the word PREGNANT.

She calls me. 'Are you crazy?' she says. 'You gave me a heart attack.' I say we need to hurry, I don't want to tell Andrea, he's going to be home soon, and I want to figure out if it's a false positive. She tells me, 'I've never heard of false positives. More like false negatives.' We start looking on all the sites in the world to see whether there's such a thing as a false positive. Andrea is due back any minute. I think: the miracle has happened. I'm sure of it: the miracle has happened. I sit on the sofa. The sun filters through the window into the room. I think, this is it, you're here. No more torture. You got here, you did it the *normal* way. I feel omnipotent.

Then my friend sends me a screenshot: usually there are no false positives. The rare few occur if you've taken chorionic gonadotropin. Which I have. But that doesn't necessarily mean it's a false positive. I did ovarian stimulation and had an injection to rupture my follicles and followed the doctor's orders on when to have sex. I'm pretending to believe it, that it's too soon, ovulation would have been a week ago and it's too fast for a test to detect a pregnancy. Though not impossible. Giulia says, 'Wait ten days or so and then check again.' 'It can't be,' I say. 'Yeah, unfortunately maybe not,' she replies. I'm pretending to believe it: all right, it didn't work.

I say nothing to Andrea. 'What's wrong?' he asks when he gets home.

And what can I say? 'Nothing.'

'You look weird.'

'Huh. No, nothing.'

I pretend to believe it, with my friend, with a doctor from a new clinic I started going to, who advised me to take another test in two weeks. OK, I'll do that. Definitely.

From the next day on, I take a test every single day. I spend hundreds of euros on them. The chorionic gonadotropin from the Gonasi will remain in my system for a minimum of ten and a maximum of fifteen days. I did the shot on the 31st. I have several days ahead of me (which I compulsively check and recheck on the calendar, counting down precisely, hoping that the more I look at them the faster they'll go by) before I'll find out if that positive is accurate or caused by the injection. I tell myself to work, and I work, all the time, I pretend to be in my right mind, but.

I'm going crazy.

I read all the online forums again, looking up Gonasi and false positives.

I've always been obsessive-compulsive.

I promise my friend I won't take another test for at least ten days.

Instead . . .

I walk to the pharmacies furthest from my house, so as not to be recognised. I rack up kilometres. I buy one test here, another there, because I'm ashamed to ask for three or four tests at a single pharmacy. I rack up kilometres and anxiety. I take one test a day. In the morning, as soon as I wake up. I resist the temptation to take two or three a day: I'm very good at that. I hide the used tests so Andrea doesn't see them. I wrap them in toilet paper and push them to the bottom of the bin. Or I put them in my bag and throw them away when I go out. I throw out all of these tests saying: pregnant, pregnant, pregnant, pregnant, pregnant, pregnant, pregnant, pregnant, pregnant. Nine times, nine days the test throws the word PREGNANT in my face, without a shadow of a doubt. Can you imagine those nine days? Waiting for the date when the Gonasi will have cleared my system. The days last for centuries and all the while I remain PREGNANT. One night I'm at a work event where I have to be interesting and charming and intelligent and I feel my underwear become damp.

I go to the bathroom. Red.

My period.

And I'm not pregnant.

Not even by the miracle of it happening when you least expect it.

There. In those nine obsessive-compulsive days, when I let the obsessive-compulsion take over, when I gave it free rein, I reached rock-bottom humiliation.

I don't tell a soul about this episode of the thousand pregnancy tests. Who could I tell who wouldn't say: you're crazy. I don't tell a soul. I think I lost my mind, in those nine days.

Yet when I go to Spain the next day and my dear friend arrives in Madrid shortly after, I'm able to have fun. I don't think about anything. I'm in Madrid. I'm with my friend. If I had been in Rome, I would have tortured myself and Andrea (without letting on the reason for it). And I would have hated him for feeling tortured. Instead, by not telling him about any of it, not making him hope as I had hoped for those nine days, not making him see for those nine days the word PREGNANT, I spared him.

He will never know about those tests. He will never know about this insanity, and this despair.

People never know what you do for them. And you never know what they do for you.

In those days in Madrid with my friend, I don't think about anything, just the fact that we are there, together.

I return to Rome, back to the horror.

When I was pregnant and then with what happened after, my parents didn't see me for several months. I found a million excuses not to go to Bari to visit them.

They must have thought I was a bad daughter (which actually I am, for other reasons). They don't know that I did it for myself, because I couldn't pretend, but also that I did it for them.

I keep quiet about so much that often people don't know what I do for them.

I wonder how much they do for me that I don't know either.

This is why, for twenty days, I couldn't write this book. Because I had to grapple with a time that was too difficult to write about – and it was real, in the past, but real – yet the reality of today, and today, and today dictates that I can never get out of that loop. When I was little, like everyone else, I had a hula hoop. The hoop keeps going around and around, you keep moving your hips, and you remain in the circle.

I don't want to be defined by these things: pregnancy in the past, pregnancy angst in the present. By this hula hoop that circles around and around that starts with pregnancy and ends with pregnancy.

That's not me.

I'm ready. Now I'm going back to that 2 February 2021.

I'm lying on the gurney in the operating room. They explain what will happen in the procedure. They've explained it before, but they explain it again.

The interns are all around, quiet. The doctor who'll be doing the operation comes in. He's nice, but I don't know him. It's silly, but I'd prefer to have only women around me now, and only women I know. The doctor who was with me through the whole process in Milan is here. She smiles at me. She squeezes my hand in encouragement. She's sitting next to the operating doctor in front of the ultrasound monitor. I see everything.

They explain step by step what's going to happen. I will be awake. I wish I could be asleep. 'Now relax.' They spread the ultrasound gel on my belly. We look. A voice in my head tells me not to look. I look. I see everything. The three of them appear in the ultrasound, lively. They move and grow. The little hearts are blue and red and beat strong. The doctor dabs a red liquid on my belly. They've decided which one they're going to *reduce*. Now, he'll give me an injection. The injection will stop the heart (I write, delete, rewrite) of the one out of the three that they have decided to *reduce*, and then they will block off the umbilical cord so that it doesn't affect the others. They aim the needle at the point where she is – where I'm supposed to protect her. Instead, I'm telling her: die. The needle sinks into my belly. I feel pain, yes, but what is pain to me now. It's nothing but a distant rumble. The doctor pushes, and pushes, and sinks the needle into my belly.

I'm an avid follower of crime news. Do you know how often a person trying to kill another is stunned because we all think you just wrap your hands around someone's neck and they die? You just stab someone with a knife and they die? I know that isn't the case. In confessions or pretrial hearings murderers will say, 'I squeezed. I pressed. He didn't die. It took forever.' But I'd never seen it, until now.

And as the doctor pushes the needle deeper into my belly, harder and harder, everyone is looking at the monitor, including me, and I see them: the three resisting hearts. She doesn't die. She struggles to die, I think. Stop watching, I beg you. I don't stop. There are these three beautiful lines on the graph, these glorious heartbeats, these beautiful lines of three hearts beating. And then. One line goes flat. The sound becomes uniform and that's death. One heart is gone.

I burst out crying. But without a sound, only tears. What happened is my fault too. It was a choice. I always could have entrusted myself to God.

They say some words of comfort, moving the ultrasound over my belly. 'Let's see how the other two are doing.'

They have to check whether suddenly all the blood, all the nutrients I've been giving them, evenly divided between the three, have killed them – whether now there are only two. Too strong a blast of blood and nourishment and mothering. But they're beating. They're lively. They're moving. If they survive, the little body of the daughter I chose to let die will remain inside me until delivery. But who am I to complain. If they survive, it's they who'll have to stay there next to their dead sister. They'll have to live with her. Now there's not five of us any more. Now we're four.

I cry and I don't stop crying when they tell me that it has gone well so far, that image burned into my brain of my daughter's heart stopping is a horror, it's not something from TV, it's a horror, it can't be real, that image of that heart stopping beating is impossible, impossible to accept.

I cry and I don't stop crying when they bring Andrea inside – almost laughably dressed in shoe covers, a green surgical cap and surgical gown – and tell him that it has gone fine so far but I need to stay there in observation, without moving an inch, for a couple of hours; I don't stop crying when Andrea comes and sits next to me, talks to me, holds my hand, and I fall asleep; I don't stop when I wake up and fall back asleep again. After two hours they examine me. The other two have held on. Those two are still there.

What is it, seeing an inert, motionless foetus, like the floating children in *It*, on a screen, without a heartbeat, no more blue or red. What is it – it's impossible. A dark spot in black and white with a head a body two arms two hands two legs that don't move any more.

The other two are all right. The other two are moving and I hope they're joking around together. I feel like they are. I convince myself that they are.

'You saw, they're fine,' Andrea says. 'Tomorrow morning at nine o'clock, come in for the ultrasound; if everything is OK you can go back to Rome.' 'We took the train, is it dangerous?' I ask. 'No no, the train is much better than driving.' This sentence heartens me. I don't know why, but it makes me think of normalcy. The two of us and our two daughters heading back to Rome.

We leave the hospital, walking very slowly. Andrea is holding me up. I don't need to be held up. I mean, I don't *physically* need to be held up. A bruise spreads across the spot where they gave me the injection in my belly.

That bruise will take a month to fade. Every time I see it it's like someone slamming your head into a wall. Go on, go crazy, they tell you. But you don't want to.

The hotel is very near, but Andrea, who by nature is always easygoing (to a fault), always even-tempered (to a fault), always kind to strangers (to a fault), leaps at a taxi and says, 'Take her to this hotel,' adding the name and address, 'please.' The driver protests: 'It's too close.' Andrea glowers menacingly, and says, 'She's had an operation. She can't walk. Take her.'

I look out at Milan, or rather I don't look out at Milan but at the people, and the streets, and the sun, and maybe I'm still out of it from the drugs because it all seems like a dream. It seems like they're in heaven. And I'm in a cab on the way to limbo.

Back the hotel I lie down. It's 5.30 p.m.

Ada: 'Hang in there. Get some rest and if you're feeling up to it, eat something good.'

Me: 'I can't. At 6.30 p.m. I have an important call about the book.'

Bianca: 'Do you have to? Can't you postpone?'

Me: 'No.'

(Of course I could, I could find a way, but I can't.)

＊

8.59 p.m.

Bianca: 'How are you doing? Have you eaten?'

Me: 'Some shitty soup at the shitty restaurant at this shitty hotel' and three LOL emojis. 'Big day.'

Bianca: 'Jesus. Time to go on a rampage.'

Me: 'I'm ready.'

Bianca: 'Fuck everybody.'

Same day, same time, with Giulia.

Her: 'Stay in bed, Antonello, and don't move an inch.' She uses the masculine version of my name, it's our thing, an expression of affection.

Me: 'I mean, I saw that little heart that was beating and now it's not any more.'

Pause. 'You were so brave. Strong. Courageous.' *Bravissima. Corragiosa.* Now she uses the feminine – how could she not?

'I thought a mother is supposed to protect. Whereas I, let's say . . .' – we always use this expression, 'let's say,' to allude to all kinds of things like, in this case: I'm an asshole.

'They wouldn't have survived, all three of them. Now they have a chance.'

'It was never-ending.' Pause. 'It felt like something from court TV, those people who say their victims wouldn't die. Like just fucking say it was murder.'

3 February, 8.40 a.m.

Ada: 'How are you? Did you sleep?'

Me: 'Yes. Anxiety dreams since time immemorial,' LOL emoji. 'Now I'm going back in for a scan' (more emojis, as always, to lighten things).

Ada: 'OK. Keep us posted.'

Me: yellow heart.

Bianca: 'And then come back to us.'

Me: 'I will.' And – I realise only now – I add a floating red balloon and two pink hearts, all in a row. I swear, I didn't mean to.

I'm in the hospital, on that exam table, to see how the two are doing. Andrea is beside me.

The doctor, trying to distract us, begins the ultrasound.

I see them, crystal clear. Those three babies, motionless, on the screen. But I can't believe it. It's not true.

She turns serious; she looks and looks again. Then: 'I'm sorry,' she says. 'They didn't make it.'

Too much blood – from me – too much nourishment – from me – all at once. I wonder if their hearts burst. They're dead.

I don't believe it. I think: now she'll see them moving.

There are the flat lines of the three hearts. There's a noise like when the radio doesn't work. White noise. Nothing else. There are flat lines. Not a blip. The dancing is done.

And Andrea. Andrea bolts up from his chair, tears off his coat, he's suffocating.

'What is it,' the doctor says.

What the fuck do you think it is, I want to say. His daughters are dead.

I cry, and cry, and ask the doctor, 'What do I do now, what do I do now.'

Andrea has gone pale. He comes over to me. He takes my hand.

She says, 'I'm so sorry. You'll have to have a D&C. But you can do it in Rome.'

*

A D&C. Like an abortion. Like the two children I didn't want. Except these three.

That image. Andrea bolting up from his chair and tearing off his coat, without a word. We've been together for almost seven years. I've never seen him so devastated. Not even with the most unbearable pain.

That image. It expresses the measure of the tragedy. It tells me that it's true. It screams that it's true. But I don't believe it's true.

3 February, 11.03 a.m.
   Me: 'All three of them died.'

Ada, Bianca, Giulia, in the various chats, reply with one word: 'No.'

And I – until now I've never told this to anyone, not even myself, least of all Andrea – at 9 a.m. on 3 February, as I went through the revolving door into the hospital, on my way to the ultrasound to see how my two remaining daughters had done through the night after the operation, I thought: hopefully only one was saved. That way she'll be safe for sure. Forever.

A horrible thought. Unforgivable.

They told us it was three girls the day before they died. Life, you're too much. How much torturous, dramatic pain are you trying to cause. I don't like melodramatic writing. And I don't like you. Why couldn't you do what you had to do in short sentences, without adjectives, without whining or sentimentalism? Why, life, couldn't you be a better writer?

Every time I finish a chapter in Word, I select the 'Break' function and then click 'Page.' Every time, I think 'heart'.

All that pain.

It's not possible, but it was still better than the total void that I am now.

Today, my Facebook memories show me that picture from last year. The one of me peeking out the door of the church next to the words: 'don't bang on your way out'. The last photo I have with them in Rome.

Whereas today, it's 2 February 2022.

The last day I can say I was with them last year.

No one remembers that it was today, and that it was this time of year. Or no one says so. Other people's lives have carried on. I'm stuck in the hula hoop. Yesterday Andrea and I watched a stupid show. A man who's been wrongfully imprisoned. His seventeen-year-old daughter goes to visit him. She's pregnant. You can already see her round belly.

I say, 'Fuck you.'

Andrea: 'Who?'

'That bitch.'

'OK, OK, come on,' he says. 'You can't keep saying that. You can't get pissed off every time. These things happen in movies. Pregnancy, death, falling in love. All that stuff.'

I say nothing more, but I go on hating her and hoping she loses that baby.

She doesn't.

Date: 2 February, 2021

Patient Information

Last name: Lattanzi   **First name:** Antonella
Date of birth: 20 November, 1979   **Age:** 41

Current pregnancy
Last menstrual period: 9 November, 2020
Gestational age (LMP): Sept. 12 + 1 day
EDD (LMP): 16 August, 2021
Gestational age (US): Sept. 12 + 5 days
EDD (US): 12 August, 2021

(these are the dates they would have been born, 16 August based on my last menstrual period, 12 August according to ultrasound)

Multiple pregnancy monochorionic triamniotic

Ultrasound
Foetus 1: Cardiac activity   visualised
Foetus 2: Cardiac activity   visualised
Foetus 3: Cardiac activity   visualised

Invasive procedures
Indication   Multifoetal pregnancy

Embryo reduction / Foeticide

Procedure   Embryo reduction
Instrument   Interstitial laser
Live foetuses before procedure   3
Live foetuses after procedure   2

Date: 3 February, 2021

Patient Information

Last name: Lattanzi   **First name:** Antonella
Date of birth: 20 November, 1979   **Age:** 41

Current pregnancy
Last menstrual period: 9 November, 2020
Gestational age (LMP): Sept. 12 + 2 days
EDD (LMP): 16 August, 2021
Gestational age (US): Sept. 12 + 6 days
EDD (US): 12 August, 2021

First Trimester Ultrasound	Foetus 1	Foetus 2	Foetus 3
Diagnosis	Foetal death	Foetal death	Foetal death
Cardiac Activity	**absent**	**absent**	**absent**

Notes:
Cardiac activity absent for all three.

Treatment:
Refer out for dilation and curettage.

(In Italian, a term used for D&C – everywhere, among doctors, on medical records – is uterine *revisione*. A *revisione* is also a tune-up, like for a car; it always made me think of that. I feel like I've become a car, that you can fix up and get back on the road. I wish I were. Even an old black Yaris like the one Andrea and I have.)

Afterwards, we take the train back to Rome. It's the two of us, me and Andrea, but I'm alone. No other hearts beating inside me.

I didn't say anything to my publisher. I can handle it. I have to keep working for the book.

That's the only thing I have left, the novel. I say it, I think it, and it's true.

I have a presentation to record live the next day, and my abdomen is very sore, but I do it. That's the presentation my mother sees that makes her say, how come you're always in a skirt?

I go to Ada's the night after I get back to Rome. Andrea is out, he's back on set, and she doesn't want me to be alone. She invites me over. Some other people are there too. 'Do you feel up to it?' she asks. What am I supposed to do. I don't feel anything.

On 3 February, back at the hotel, I called Dr S., crying desperately. 'My dear Antonella, I can't tell you how sorry I am,' he said, his voice breaking.

What's keeping me alive? The novel. Everyone who knows about it tells me: now rest, then you can try again, try for another baby. But those three are dead. They're gone forever. The novel keeps me alive, it becomes everything: my three daughters and my work and my hope and my ambition. Books aren't children, as I said. But everything that persuades me not to throw myself out of my sixth-floor window is there, in those nearly four hundred pages.

And I can't rest now. Not even psychologically. I have to get the D&C.

I had a dream.

A stupid, didactic dream; I always have didactic dreams. I dreamed of the sea in Sabaudia, and it was all red. The sun was setting. It wasn't crystal-clear water. It was an endless sea of blood, all the way to the horizon.

I had this dream because the bleeding has begun. It will culminate on a night in June up in Circeo. As I said, my dreams are simplistic.

Now what can I tell you?

That I tasked my book with the responsibility of keeping me alive?

That when I had to go to hospital to have the ultrasound for the D&C, there were pregnant women everywhere. I could hear the baby heartbeats pumping loudly from behind closed doors.

That before going in, I was embarrassed, but I said to Andrea, 'Maybe now we'll do the scan and they'll be alive.' And he said, 'I had the same thought' (out of our minds).

That I went in for a curettage of three dead foetuses over twelve weeks old, and at first they told me that I would have to give birth to them, dead, go through labour, because there were too many of them and the pregnancy was too far along.

That at that point, I lost it.

*

That the curettage went badly, I lost two litres of blood, I was losing my uterus, I went through everything imaginable, catheter, transfusion, uterine packing to stop the haemorrhaging, plummeting haemoglobin, risk of sepsis. That the cruel nurses wouldn't give me water after the surgery, that I begged and finally they gave me some from the tap, but for a cup they used a baby bottle because they'd put me in Obstetric Pathology.

It was nighttime. I hadn't eaten since midnight the previous day. I asked for something to eat, my stomach was aching. They said, 'We'll try to find you some crackers.' 'Please,' I begged. 'OK,' they said. They never came back.

For the bleeding, they gave me nappies for babies.

What can I say?

That, before the curettage, they asked me if I wanted to baptise my three baby girls? If I wanted a place for them in the children's cemetery. I wanted to open my mouth and clamp onto that obstetrician's jugular. Not even dead would I entrust them to God.

That before we entered the operating room, they said to Andrea, 'Daddy has to go now, he can't stay.' *Daddy?* Like a big rusty nail being hammered into your brain. *Daddy, Mummy.* In these places they keep on calling you father and mother even when you've lost your children, even when you aren't a mother or father any more. The nurses and the obstetricians call you that constantly. Every time they do, you envy (you hate) anyone who can rightfully answer to that name. And you wonder: Do these people have any idea what they're saying?

That it was still bloody Covid, and I had to stay in

hospital for a week without being able to have visitors, not even Andrea. I was alone, in pain, weak, with an excruciating headache and a high fever. Next to me, in the bed next to mine, was a twenty-year-old girl from Macedonia, six months pregnant with her third child. And they would come to listen to the heartbeat right there in the room.

That at night, every night, she would have a headache that paralysed half her body and made her nose bleed, and even though I hated her because she was pregnant, I would call the nurses for her. They never came. Eventually, even though I couldn't bear it, even though my haemoglobin was down to 6, even though I couldn't get up – I would get up. It wasn't out of kindness, empathy, or pity. I did it because it had to be done. I went down the hall. I wanted to scream at the nurses, get your asses over here, you fucking bitches. Instead, I politely approached those nurses who held our lives in their hands, our pain medications, our only connection to the world and to the doctors, a power over us as if we were in prison, and politely and nicely I would say, My roommate needs help, could you please come? They didn't come.

That the day after the curettage, the female doctor on duty looked at me and said, 'You deserved for the curettage to go badly.' Because I refused an induction to deliver dead foetuses, because I was at a Catholic hospital and I wasn't one of them – assisted reproduction, the reduction – and I didn't deserve anything.

That Andrea called my friends, my best friends who didn't know any of it, and told them. Luca, Emilio and Carlo, Marco. And they couldn't believe I had kept all of this secret, and they texted me and wanted to be there with me in the hospital.

That I didn't make those calls to my friends who didn't know, I had Andrea call them. Because I couldn't talk to anybody. I never answered phone calls. I communicated exclusively via text.

That Giulia, Ada and Bianca checked in with Andrea every day, and wanted to come even though they knew I couldn't see them, they couldn't come in. Fucking Covid. Fucking world. Fucking everything.

That when we realised that I was going to be hospitalised for a while, Andrea called my publisher and explained everything. I was in hospital and at that point, that week, for the first time, I had to tell the truth. I had to stop. Their stunned messages. When I got home, I called the publisher myself. They tested the ground, what do you say, how does one react to a loss like this? Stop, they told me. Don't think about the book, it's well on its way, you're not needed. Take a week, a month, a year. All the time you want. You need to focus on yourself. And I said, 'I can't stop if I have to focus on myself. If I don't work on the book, I'll die.' And they – understanding me or not – left it up to me. Starting the afternoon I came home from hospital, haemoglobin at 7, I resumed the online presentations and interviews, where each time I was asked: so, do you have kids?

I set out to write an essay on Stephen King. My editor for that project didn't know anything about what had happened (it was a different publisher than for my novel), and he still doesn't know. It's an ebook called *Salvarsi*, saving yourself, which is not a coincidence.

Months later, when I went back to Dr S. for the

thousandth time, begging him to start me on another round of IVF, without the slightest regard for my body or mind, he told me, warmly, 'Be gentle with yourself.'

Gentle how?

And on the way home I was crying and thinking: I have to try again. And the Tiber was black.

What can I say?
   That when I was in the hospital, desperate, a priest entered my room? I was crying and crying, and he thought it was because I wanted his blessing. All I wanted was him out of that room, I wanted him mauled by lions, but I was nothing, I was nothing at all, I let him violate me because I was nothing, all I did was cry, and he said, 'Were they boys?' I nodded, crying, and he said, 'Baptise the three dead babies, name them after the archangels, and make a donation to – he named a place, a church, I don't remember which – and I promise that within a year you'll be pregnant again.' And he gave me a necklace: a Franciscan cross. And I cried and thought, they were girls, at least you didn't take that from me.

I threw away the cross as soon as I got out of the hospital. I was afraid to get rid of it there. I was afraid it would bring misfortune; I was afraid I would die in there.

Should I say that, on the day I went for the D&C, I took a taxi because the potholes in Rome were too much for me on the scooter, and Andrea took the scooter because he was only staying for a little bit and then going on set? The taxi got a flat tire. I couldn't believe it. The driver left me on the side of a huge road, practically a highway, and said, 'Call another taxi.'

Many times in that hospital they promised us that they would give me a room by myself, without all these pregnant women, without all these beating hearts, but no, I was with the super-pregnant Macedonian the whole time, and I had a catheter and a Tylenol drip – very little, because pain comes from God – along with antibiotics and fluids and little tubes all over, and the bleeding and the gauze in my uterus, and they told me, you might lose your uterus (too) you might lose it you might lose your uterus you might lose it you almost lost it and we almost lost you too.

The IV bag with the transfusion, filled with blood, was dark red. It was never ending. My haemoglobin wouldn't go up.

What can I say?
That an obstetrician said to me, 'This is a horrendous thing you're going through. But you have to accept it and embrace it. God only brings pain to those who can bear it.'

That after the curettage, I remained in delivery under observation all day, alone, because I had lost too much blood, while babies were being born all around me.

That right after the curettage was the only time they gave me something for the pain besides Tylenol. That was the only time they gave me morphine. And I, who hadn't told anyone anything, because I thought I would be out of there by afternoon – after all, I'd had a D&C twice before, I thought I knew what it would be like, which is also what the doctors told me – on morphine I felt almost euphoric, and I replied to texts about work without saying a word about where I was or what I was doing, I answered emails, super-excited, and the publisher wrote to me: 'We just found out that your book is going into a second printing.' And I reported the news to Ada and Bianca. They replied, 'Fantastic!' My poor sweet friends.

That, before the curettage, as with any other surgery, I had to go in for a preoperative evaluation. Giulia took me to the pre-op and, two days prior, to the scan when they told me I'd have to induce labour. Andrea couldn't come. Andrea didn't want to come; it was a relief for him not to come (hey, don't be unfair). On the day of the ultrasound, when they recommend induction, Giulia becomes a crusader. She calls everyone she knows while I cry and cry and cry, I say if I have to give birth to my three dead daughters I'll die too; Giulia, my friend, calls doctors, friends of doctors, the children of head physicians, finally managing to reach the head physicians themselves. I sit in the cold outside the hospital smoking a million cigarettes because everyone is dead now anyway. I sit on the ground because I can't bear it, while I watch her making calls and think, Andrea would never have done this for me. You call, he would've said. Because if Andrea were a character in a novel, he couldn't be a zealous crusader like Giulia and be himself at the same time.

Giulia calls all over and finds a way to help me – which means I won't deliver by induction – then she takes me home and we drink a bunch of beers. We're all dead now anyway. We manage to talk about other things too. We even manage to laugh.

When, around eleven at night, Andrea gets home from set, I hate him. Because he doesn't have to have surgeries. Because he's a man. Because he can go out into the world and I'm stuck inside mine. Because he, if I couldn't have children, could have them, for decades still, with other women. He says, 'I got your favourite, fish and mussels' (it can't be eleven if he came home with fish, maybe he says that the next day, arriving earlier, around eight, but since the next day is identical to this one, let's not worry about how things went *exactly*). I turn cold, mean, I say: 'What the fuck do I care about mussels' (my favourite food). 'I'm not hungry.'

On the day of my pre-op exam, while I'm waiting to go in, Andrea and I are fighting on WhatsApp. We're always fighting. It's freezing cold, it's February, and I stand in the queue outside for hours because with Covid only a certain number of people are allowed in. While I'm here, he's out living. For days I've had three dead babies inside me. I've been going around with three dead babies inside.

I do a reading immediately after the procedure in Milan, before the D&C, carrying three dead babies. Between going back to Rome, the appointments, and the curettage, I spend seven full days with three dead baby girls inside me.

In the pre-op room I sit there waiting I don't know how long to get my blood taken, do a Covid test, and have my consultation with the anaesthetist. (Previous anaesthesia? No. Previous pregnancies? No. Previous surgeries? No). I arrive at the hospital at nine in the morning and get back home at seven in the evening.

Two days before, when we were waiting to do the ultrasound, the nurses would close the doors every so often and say, Stay back, Covid patient coming through. I didn't think: at least I don't have Covid.

Because at a certain point this thing happened.

It started in December 2020, when I was afraid I was carrying twins. As soon as I'd say, at least *this* didn't happen, it would happen. When I was afraid I wouldn't make it to the third month – in the period when I thought I was having a normal pregnancy, and like any normal woman I was worried – I said, at least I can be sure of one thing, it's not twins. As soon as I said it I found out there were two. Then I thought, at least it's not three. And they became three. When I went in for the curettage I thought, at least I'll be back home by tonight. And I didn't get back home for a week. After the curettage, they told me, you could've lost your uterus. I said, at least I didn't lose my uterus, at least my uterus is all right. And that was when the second part of this tragedy began.

I commanded myself not to say anything more, not to think anything more, not to emit the slightest noise either out loud or in my head. From heaven to hell they hear you, always listening, punishing you. So I stayed silent. Because anyway in my head there was only one sound.

The hearts of those babies.

When they became three, under the terrified gaze of the doctor who guided me through fertility treatment,

I fucking saw those tiny things and heard those hearts beating so hard, I fucking saw them pulsing blue and red on the ultrasound, and despite the gynaecologist laying out a death scenario before me, I don't know what it is, the heartbeat of a baby you want, something like total warmth, a narcotic, an explosion. I would discover that the heartbeat of other babies, if you've lost your own, is a form of torture. Like being tied to a chair and getting your skull opened and your brain carved up with a razor. You're conscious, but you're going insane. You think: make those hearts stop. Please, I'm begging you, get those hearts to stop.

And you're a horrible person, you're a horrible person to think that if your hearts have died, then everyone else's should, and these are little children. You will think that you're a horrible person, you will think that you deserve the worst of all punishments, you will think that these are the thoughts of a murderer, not of a normal person. And you'll tell Andrea, please, make those hearts stop. And he'll say, on the phone, because there's Coronavirus and he can't come into hospital with you, he'll say not to talk that way, what did those little babies do to you. And he'll be right, and you'll know it. But you would do anything to get those hearts to stop, yet you keep hearing them, every second, in the Obstetric Pathology unit you're in after the thousandth operation, and there's no one left inside you when the ultrasound wand goes in, no more Aldo, Giovanni and Giacomo, as you called them when you first found out there were three (before knowing that they were girls, who didn't have a chance to each have a name, and before they became two, Annalena Angela and Bianca Cristina – serious names, this time); there's nothing left inside you, you're no longer yourself, and you hear these hearts and you want to rip the catheter out of you, the ten metres of gauze stuffed inside you to stop your uterus from haemorrhaging, the IV with liquids and the IV with Tylenol and the IV with antibiotics because you got a fever and they say they have to make sure you don't go into septic shock, and the red IV with the blood transfusion. You want to rip everything out and run as far away as you can, and unfortunately, this time, it's not like when Giulia said to you, laughing, You can't run away, where would you go? They're inside you. Unfortunately this time you can run away. If you run away you'll be alone. Nobody is with you any more.

And that dimension you plummeted into on 3 February 2021, the day your daughters died, that dimension you're still stuck in keeps telling you, every day, every hour, that it wasn't misfortune, or bad luck, like everyone says, or even fate. No, only one thing is certain: you deserved it. A child isn't an outfit, it isn't a book contract, it's not an unregistered deed to a beach house; you rejected two children and so the finger you'd always expected finally came down from the sky and pierced the clouds, tensed and muscular, pointing you out to the world and saying: you. You don't deserve this. And it killed your three little girls.

Before releasing me, they have me lie back on the table so they can pull the gauze out of my uterus. They don't say a word to me.

They pull out metres and metres of gauze, it never seems to end, and it makes an awful noise.

Immediately, I feel a gush of liquid flow out of my body. The gauze was there to stop the bleeding.

'What's going on?' I ask, while I can't see what's happening to my lower half. 'What's going on?' I ask the doctors. Nobody responds.

'Am I bleeding? Am I still bleeding?'

It's a lot of liquid, and it starts pooling.

Finally they decide to speak: 'No, it's the disinfectant we soak the gauze in. We have to use a lot.'

Should I really say these things? These are things that go unspoken, things so simple you have to experience them firsthand, as Simenon says in *The Blue Room*. So be it.

I won't say them.

Do you know what I have to say instead?

During those never-ending days in the hospital, I don't want to hear anyone with a happy voice, I want everyone to die. But time stands still. I can't read, I can only watch movies or TV on my phone. Every day, a thousand hours a day, I google, 'movies with unhappy endings' and only watch those. Other people's suffering is my gratification. When I get out of the hospital, I tell this to Giulia. She laughs. It makes me want to laugh too.

The Macedonian girl I shared the hospital room with, when she and I were discharged (we were discharged at the same time), and I got dressed to leave, she looked at my outfit (purchased ages ago from a very chic boutique, because I aspire to be that put-together woman) and said, 'You look like a gypsy.' It really pissed me off. When I told my friends they laughed. So did I.

After I was discharged, dragging myself down the corridors towards the hospital exit I muttered, 'Can you believe that bitch telling me these are fucking gypsy clothes with all the money I spent on them.' And Andrea looked around and said, 'Hey, lower your voice, you can't say that.' At the time it didn't seem funny. Now it does.

*

One time, the umpteenth time the nurses didn't answer when we called them, didn't bring us our painkiller drips, didn't bring our blankets, I started shouting, 'I'm a journalist, you know! I'm going to write all this in the paper and ruin you!' with the idea that they would be intimidated by my authority and treat me much better. They treated me worse. In the end, my friends and I laughed about this, too. 'They didn't give two shits,' they told me. It's true, they didn't.

And then there are other things to tell.

I have a note on my iPhone. It has got very long. It has the dates of all my rounds of IVF. When I started it, I thought it would have ten lines at most. One line for each date: when I started, when I went in for monitoring, when I had the retrieval, when I had the transfer, when I found out I was pregnant, when I gave birth. The end.

You make me laugh, Antonella (you're an idiot, that's why I'm calling you by your full name which you hate).

Now the list is very long. It takes several seconds to scroll all the way through.

I look at the date I went into the hospital for the D&C: 10 February 2021. I got out on the 17th.

Andrea picks me up, exhausted. He spent almost every minute he wasn't on set sitting in the hallway outside the unit (they wouldn't let him in, they promised information they never provided, and if I didn't answer his messages – I didn't want to talk to him on the phone, either – no one would tell him how I was). Finally, I get dressed (in my gypsy garb), throw my stuff in my suitcase, and slowly walk out.

*

(I only find out once I'm home that while I was in delivery for the curettage, someone stole the diamond bracelet my mother and father had given me from their retirement bonus: one for me, one for my sister. 'Why didn't you take it off before you went into hospital? You can't wear jewellery there.' I know this, and I had no earrings or rings, but I hadn't taken the bracelet off for fifteen years, it was just there, I didn't even remember.)

We walk down endless hospital corridors. I'm out of breath. Andrea is holding me tight. There are signs on the walls saying that suffering comes from the Lord. To which I just say, fuck you. We get to the exit. Just outside the hospital there's a bookstore. I glance at it. There's a stack of books in the window. In the middle of this stack, right in the middle, in the most prominent spot, I see my novel.

These, yes, these are the things you tell. This moment of true, total light amid the fluorescent lights of the hospital, this suitcase full of horrors that Andrea is pulling for me, this cab that takes me home while Andrea rides the scooter, this nullity that I've become. These are the things you tell: that novel, which has been there this whole time, standing guard, waiting for me. Waiting to tell me that I'm still alive.

Forgive me, novel, for tasking you with saving my life.

And starting that day I come home from hospital, my publisher and I talk about translations in other languages, reprints, sales, new projects, interviews, readings (online for the week, then back to live).

Right away there's a recording where I look ghastly (I tell my publicist, 'I look like Morticia'). But I laugh, I laugh so much in that event, I want to show them – my publisher, but most of all myself – how good I am, how brave I am, and when I'm asked: Do you have kids? I reply with a smile: No!

(What's a novel in the face of all this pain? Nothing.

Why do I keep on working nonstop?

Why will I always do this, given everything that is still to happen?

An image comes to mind: a hand clinging to the side of a cliff, a body dangling in the void. The hand is giving out, it can't last much longer. Maybe this is what it means: make sure to have something to hold on to.

That this something kept me from having children sooner, that it led me here, to these three deaths, these three killings, should mean calling it into question. Yet I can't, because that would bring me to a total lack of meaning.

I never call it into question, ever, not even as I'm writing now.

Never. I don't even want to think about it. I want to delete this chapter.)

But now I have to talk about the blood.

Summary:

Immediately after the D&C, I have some bleeding. The doctors assume it's normal post-op recovery. So do I. At least I didn't lose my uterus (Shh! Don't think it!). However, it turns out that in order to save my uterus and stop the initial bleeding, the doctors at the hospital had to finish the operation quickly. Remnants of the dead foetuses and the placenta were left behind inside my uterus. Arteriovenous formations grew on those remains. That is, living, growing blood vessels and arteries (I'm not a doctor, I explain as best I can). From February to June 2021, they grow out of control. All the doctors tell me this is very rare, that this never happens. But this whole story is about the zero-point-zero-zero-one per cent chance that always fucking seems to come true. In the scans my uterus is completely filled with little coloured dots. These are not babies' hearts. They are blood vessels spurting blood. The hospital wants to bring me back in early April for an emergency operation ('to save your life,' they say). We go for a medical consultation: the operation is deemed too risky. There is a very high probability of losing my uterus. A high probability of not being able to stop the bleeding even by removing the uterus, and therefore that I would die. I ask the doctors what to do. They advise me not to have the operation, they say we'll try other treatments, we'll try every type of treatment in existence. I refuse the operation.

*

We try various treatments to shrink this mass – it's called an AVM, arteriovenous malformation – in order to operate on it later. For months and months, my haemoglobin plummets and blood pours out of me.

I still go out for events, work, to dinner. My blood pays no attention to the haemostatic (500 mg Tranex). I can haemorrhage at any moment. It happens all the time. All over the place. In the middle of whatever I'm doing, I'll feel a gush of blood and have to run to the bathroom. Down a bunch of Tranex. Pray it stops. Every time, it could be fatal. My gynaecologist and I are in touch every minute. 'Bleeding is serious. If it's too much, go to hospital.' Logic tells me to barricade myself in bed and never move again. Everything is too dangerous. But I get out of that bed every morning. And not out of courage. Because I don't want it to be true. If you don't believe it, it's not happening.

I go on like this through to the end of June. I have a packed schedule of readings and events from spring to summer. It was my doing. I keep going out, travelling, doing events. For months. On haemostatics and the rest.

I keep leaving, keep travelling, doing events. For months and months. With antihaemorrhagics and all.

Then we get the house in Circeo, 'to recuperate'. And then comes the day I described at the beginning of this book, when the bleeding doesn't stop.

At that point, Dr S. tells me: 'Go to A&E.' I can't give in to panic. My heart is pounding against my chest, though from the outside I seem completely calm.

Andrea appears calm as well. But when he goes to shut the bag he threw together, he can't do it. I can see his hands shaking. He can't get the zipper closed. 'Don't worry,' he says, 'we're leaving.' 'Don't worry,' I reply, 'we have plenty of time.' And we, who like a couple of lunatics had gone and holed up in the most inconvenient and isolated place in the world, dash into the night up the Pontina, while I tell Andrea, relax, don't speed, we'll make it.

We tried everything we could to avoid surgery, to save my uterus so that I could start another round of fertility treatment; stubborn and reckless as I am, I always swore there wasn't too much blood, and now we have to rush. There's no sense in bleeding to death.

It's night, we are on the Pontina, full of potholes. Andrea is speeding like a madman.

But before this, 22 March 2021, the twelve Strega finalists are announced.

We've made it to this day on all our efforts and enthusiasm, me ignoring the blood (which I didn't mention to the publisher, otherwise they wouldn't have allowed me to travel; I don't tell them until June, when the surgery becomes inevitable). As I said, I tasked the novel with saving me. Here was the culmination: the twelve finalists for the Strega.

We meet on Zoom to listen together, live, to the announcement of the twelve books that have been chosen. Me at home; my publisher in Milan.

I sit at the screen. Andrea paces back and forth through the house, he doesn't want to be in the frame. We're all transfixed.

(My redemption.)

The announcement goes on for few minutes. Then: we didn't make it.

And I relive the moment I saw my three daughters dead on the screen. It's not comparable, but it's another dream that died in front of a screen. And as he did when he got me mussels and fish the day before the D&C, Andrea buys me flowers and says, 'How can I make it better?'

But I'm irate. 'There's nothing you can do,' I hiss angrily. I hate those flowers of defeat. Get the fuck out of here, you, all of you.

I don't know how easy it is to understand this, but if you work your whole life towards a certain thing, a day, an announcement – if the only reason you don't throw open that sixth floor window is that day, that announcement – when you see it all unravel on the screen, you say to yourself: It's the universe, the universe has it in for me.

And the bleeding persists until that June night on the Pontina.

I won't say what happens between that night on the Pontina and the operation. Those are weeks in which we learn that I may never leave those operating rooms again (but I had to go, I had no choice). I won't get into the operation either. It's actually two procedures in one day: an embolisation and an operative hysteroscopy (I won't explain what these are).

These are things that must go unspoken.

What I can say:

When the surgery becomes inevitable, everyone who knows does everything they can to help me find the best hospital. Eventually, for various reasons, I have to go back to the hospital where I had the curettage. But even then, everyone helps me out.

We decide to pay for a private room so that Andrea can stay with me and I won't have to deal with roommates or heartbeats. We go into hospital on Sunday night; my surgery is on Tuesday.

That Sunday, Andrea goes back home to sleep. I spend the evening on WhatsApp with the friend I'll meet in Madrid the next year, laughing at all the stupid stuff we can think of. For example, there's a button for a reading light on the side of the bed. It's supposed to turn off the other lights and turn on a dim spotlight for you to read. Instead, when you push the button, everything goes dark. All the lights go out. I send her a bunch of black pictures saying, Sorry, I have to go, I'm going to read now. We crack up, her at home, me at the hospital.

The day before the operation, I can't drink or eat after midnight. I ask Andrea to bring two Peronis to the hospital (I'm from Bari, I drink Peroni). We sneak an aperitivo with crisps and Peroni in my hospital room. As soon as we hear footsteps approaching the door, we hide everything. We laugh and laugh.

Not for an instant do I think I might die.

The next day, when they're getting ready for the first procedure, I hear the surgeon tell the assistant, 'The patient is thin, it will be easier to operate.' I'm very proud of this compliment.

That night, after the operations, I'm pumped full of morphine. But I'm awake. I buy the Monopoly app and force Andrea to play a million times on my iPhone. It's fiddly and tedious. Despite the pain and the morphine I win every time. I'm jubilant.

('I let you win, actually,' Andrea will tell me months later, and I'll laugh.)

I have a self-administering IV for the morphine, so I can pump it directly into my veins (the pain from these two operations is beyond anything I've ever experienced). I finish it in no time. When the duty doctor comes to check on me and the bag is already empty I ask for more. He gives it to me, but says, 'More than this and we'll have to call Substance Abuse Services.'

That makes me proud, too.

The night I come home from the hospital, Giulia and Luca come over for dinner. I am sore, weak, but I want them there. I can barely get off the sofa. Yet I can't stop cracking jokes. 'Even after all this you're still an ass, Antonio,' Giulia tells me. I'm proud to be an ass despite it all, and she is also proud – and relieved – that I am.

When we're discharged from hospital, the duty doctor advises me to go to the sea. I am more dead than alive and afraid to leave Rome. 'What if I start bleeding again?' 'Come back here,' she says. Andrea says to me, 'Are you up to it?' I'm up to it. I always am.

They manage to save me. They manage to save my uterus.

Months later, the gynaecologist with whom I'm trying IVF again (unsuccessfully) will say to me, 'Now I can tell you, a few months before you went in for the embolisation and operative hysteroscopy, a woman with the same clinical profile as you died after the same procedure.' That's why they did everything possible to avoid the operation.

But I'm alive.

It feels like every two seconds Andrea and I stumble upon twins, the word 'twin' or actual twins in the flesh.

For example, the beach club we go to in Sabaudia is called *Gemelli*. It's clearly run by twins.

Every evening at sunset, I order an aperitivo of Dixi crisps and Spritz from one of them.

I can never tell them apart.

I've always loved the sea.

But this August sea, blindingly bright, so full of summer, of joy, is painful.

There are pregnant women all over the place.

There are children all over the place.

There is happiness all over.

This sea, this heat, this happiness – I hate it.

The only time I'm happy is in the evening, when the sun goes down – I who have always loved light and warmth – and it gets dark, like me.

I make some new friends in Sabaudia. They don't know anything about anything that happened, but we dance, we laugh, and by the fact of their existence, they save me. This story is full of people who save me without knowing it. In the evening, we cook and get drunk on chilled white wine and sing Venditti, Baglioni, Battisti, Lunapop, Jovanotti. Our favourite song is 'Notte prima degli esami'. Andrea and I decide to move from Circeo to Sabaudia and rent a cheap place near theirs for the rest of summer, until the end of August.

When August ends, I beg to stay through September and work from there. I know Andrea would prefer to go back to Rome, but he agrees.

If I go back to Rome, I . . .

'Even though they are dead, your three little girls are always with you.'

No, you'll never get me. I will never say or think 'the five of them are always with me'. Because they're not.

It takes a few months to determine whether the operation was successful. We have to see how the uterus responds. If the AVM grows back. If the uterus has really been saved.

We have to wait for my period to come back (the period that came back, months later, the day after I started this book).

Once it has come back, I have to go in for a hysteroscopy to check. It's November 2021.

Giulia: 'What are you doing?'

Me: 'I just had a hysteroscopy.'

'Did they give you the results yet?'

'No.' Pause. 'I'm waiting.'

'What are they looking for?'

'If there are adhesions or remnants or any other issues caused by the operations.' (We will always wonder whether the AVM was caused by something they did wrong during the D&C; and in fact the doctor doing my hysteroscopy says it's likely, but very difficult to prove.) Pause. 'If I can try again.' Implicitly: go through IVF again, but we don't say that.

Twenty minutes later.

I send her a picture of the report. It says:

Indication: Post-uterine artery embolisation cavity check for AVM and operative hysteroscopy for post-abortion residuals. ART

Cervical canal: normal
Uterine cavity: normal
Endometrium: proliferative
Tubal ostia: visualised normal
Biopsy: no

Notes: Hysteroscopy negative. Cavity appears normal without post-abortive residuals or synechiae.

I said: 'The doctor who did my hysteroscopy had a weird look on his face. I said: Are you angry? He said: No, I'm not angry, I'm sorry about the hell you went through. It wasn't Dr S, he was someone I'd never seen before.'

Before he did the hysteroscopy, as I was undressing and telling him what had happened and he was going through my massive pile of reports and medical records, the doctor said, 'How can you still come to doctors after everything you've been through? How can you stand it?' I replied, 'Well, what else can I do?'

What else can I do?

I can live with this pain that is the past and this pain that is the present, I can try to pretend to laugh or even, sometimes, laugh wholeheartedly, or I can kill myself.

I don't kill myself.

9 February 2022. Today.

For over a year, from the moment I found out I was pregnant until now, I've kept my last IVF shot in the fridge, hoping (when I was pregnant) that I wouldn't need it any more because everything would work out, and in fact confident that I wouldn't need it any more. It expired, and I still kept it there. Today, I threw it out.

Yesterday Marco was over for dinner. At one point he said his stomach was bothering him a little. He asked me if I had something to help. Without a word, I got up and went to get the Brioschi that Andrea bought me when I was pregnant and nauseous. The bottle was half-finished.

I picked it up. I looked at it. I thought: now I'm going to tear this place apart.

I didn't tear anything.

I put two Brioschi tablets in a glass of water and stirred it around until it dissolved, like when I was pregnant and nauseous. I didn't drink it. I took it to Marco. I don't need it any more.

I wanted to say, 'I used to drink this when . . .' But I can't because: what could he say to me? How would he react?

Every day when I take a shower, I see a scar on my groin.

It's from one of the two operations I had after the curettage, the embolisation.

It's a hole.

Each time, I forget it's there. Each time I see it, I feel myself start to crumble.

One day, I hope, it'll be part of me just like my other scars. One day it won't break me any more.

After the D&C, I no longer want to have sex. For months, I can't, and even if I could, it doesn't cross my mind. February, March, April, May, June, July. At a certain point I could, but I don't want to.

If Andrea even touches me, I want to kill him.

One night back at home, I hear the sound of the sea, as I do every night. I realise that it doesn't scare me any more. It's true, I can't sleep at night, but at least I'm not scared by the noise.

I undress for bed, and that's when I realise I'm ready.

I can try. I can try to let someone inside me. I can do it.

After everything that happened I'm scared the first time. But it's a fluid sensation – powerful. The blood throbs in my temples and I can't think any more.

Three

September 2022. I went back to Sabaudia.

The sea.

When I started this book, in November 2021, I believed I would be able to give it a happy ending. Always that absurd, enduring hope, that obtuse conviction that isn't green but black.

I've learned in these months that I can't give the book the happy ending I had hoped for. I can't end it with: 'And now, as I write, I can finally say it: there's a heart is beating inside me, and it's not my own.'

I'll probably never be able to say that.

I've learned in these months that in order to tell this story I had to change the way I write and allow myself words like 'heart' and 'love' that I usually never use. Just as I never allow myself to talk about the things that are held back by that dam. As I was writing, I said to myself: I'm used to creating a narrative arc, a hero's journey, the challenges a hero faces and succeeds at or fails – what do I do with this? How can I write this book? I had to surrender, and change.

I've never written books that end well. As I was writing, I realised that I had to rethink the idea of the happy ending, and especially what a happy ending is for this story.

*

I won't be fooled, I'll never say 'these little girls are always with me'. Because they're not.

Yet I think about them every day. About what might have been. Every day I think about what it would be like if they were here. Every day I think about wanting a child. Every blessed minute, every blessed second. About what might have been.

The sun is setting.

The June and July and August sea pained me this year too. With its joy and light that excluded me so completely.

The September sea is breaking my heart. But it's a bittersweet heartbreak. The sun blazes and dives into the sea. The colour of the sea is different, melancholy. The colour of the sky is different, unsettled.

The wind riles the waves and the sea is angry, like me.

I drink my beer, alone, looking out at the sea, until the sun sets, until it gets dark, and long after.

Andrea and my friends write, 'When are you joining us?' I can never tear myself away from the sea. I never want to leave it again. I'm someone who usually hates being alone, and I spend hours and hours quietly watching the September sea. That sea that's angry like me.

I look at it, all that water, and as I look that fiery orb of sun being engulfed by sea and the wind rising and falling flow in and out of me like something sexual.

I never want to leave this place. I look at the sea until I can't see it any more, until I can't see anything at all.

*

I'm almost done with my book. Just a few lines to go.

I won't be fooled, I'll never say 'these little girls are always with me'. Because they're not.

But there are moments like this. This one right now. I can feel the adrenaline coursing through me. Not blood: adrenaline. Gushing.

I want so much adrenaline it bursts my brain.

Welcome back, adrenaline. Fill me, fathom me, invade me, drown me.

This book has been translated thanks to a translation grant awarded by the Italian Ministry of Foreign Affairs and International Cooperation.

Questo libro è stato tradotto grazie a un contributo alla traduzione assegnato dal Ministero degli Affari Esteri e della Cooperazione Internazionale italiano.

Also translated by Jamie Richards

The Hunger of Women, Marosia Castaldi, And Other Stories

Blue Hunger, Viola di Grado, Scribe

Adua, Igiaba Scego, Jacaranda Books

Celestia, Manuele Fior, Fantagraphics

Brief Lives of Idiots, Ermanno Cavazzoni, Wakefield

Coming soon from Akoya

FICTION

La Playa, Marina Perezagua, translated by Robin Myers

Hafni Says, Helle Helle, translated by Martin Aitken

NON-FICTION

Gravity, Ada d'Adamo, translated by Alex Valente

Global Sex: What Sex Workers Know About Love and Capitalism, Sine Plambech, translated by Michael Favala Goldman

Reading the Waves, Lidia Yuknavitch

ESSAYS

The Wilderness, Ayşegül Savaş

Akoya Publishing
222 Kensal Road, London, W10 5BN

Paperback ISBN 978-1-83675-002-4
Ebook ISBN 978-1-83675-015-4

Design by Holly Titchener
Text design by Phil Cleaver
Typeset in 10/13pt Egizio URW by Six Red Marbles UK,
Thetford, Norfolk
Printed and bound in the UK by CPI Group (UK) Ltd,
Croydon, CR0 4YY

1 3 5 7 9 10 8 6 4 2

akoyapublishing.com